Tara was reduced only to the feathered silk of Marc's touch, the hand at her nape cradling her skull, fingers woven into the lush tresses of her hair.

It was like that lingering wrist kiss all, all over again—but a thousand, a million times more so. A thousand, a million sensations fluttered within her, the sheer velvet sensuality of his kiss, his mouth moving on hers, tasting her, exploring her, taking all that she was, helpless, helpless to resist... The heady scent of his aftershave, his body, was in her senses, the closeness of him, as he shaped her mouth to his.

She felt herself leaning into him, to let her own hands glide around the strong column of his back, feeling the play of muscle and sinew, only the sheerest cotton of his shirt to separate her palms from the warmth of his flesh.

She could not stop, would not—blood was surging in her, her pulse soaring. She was drowning into his kiss, unable to stop herself, to draw away, to find the sanity she so, so needed to find...

D1041163

Julia James lives in England and adores the peaceful verdant countryside and the wild shores of Cornwall. She also loves the Mediterranean—so rich in myth and history, with its sunbaked landscapes and olive groves, ancient ruins and azure seas. "The perfect setting for romance!" she says. "Rivaled only by the lush tropical heat of the Caribbean—palms swaying by a silver-sand beach lapped by turquoise waters...what more could lovers want?"

Books by Julia James

Harlequin Presents

Visit the Author Profile page
at Harlequin.com for more titles.

Julia James

BILLIONAIRE'S
MEDITERRANEAN
PROPOSAL

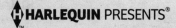

Recycling programs
for this product may
not exist in your area.

ISBN-13: 978-1-335-47832-0

Billionaire's Mediterranean Proposal

First North American publication 2019

Copyright © 2019 by Julia James

This edition published by arrangement with Harlequin Books S.A.

For questions and comments about the quality of this book, please contact us at CustomerService@Harlequin.com.

Printed in U.S.A.

BILLIONAIRE'S MEDITERRANEAN PROPOSAL

For Joyce

CHAPTER ONE

TARA SASHAYED INTO the opulent function room at the prestigious West End hotel along with the rest of the models fresh off the catwalk. They were still gowned in their couture evening dresses, and their purpose now was to show them off up close to the private fashion show's wealthy guests.

As she passed the sumptuous buffet she felt her stomach rumble, but ignored it. Like it or not—and she didn't—modelling required gruelling calorie restriction to keep her body racehorse-slender. Eating normally again would be one of the first joys of chucking in her career and finally moving to the countryside, as she was longing to do. And that dream of escape was getting closer and closer—escape to the chocolate-box, roses-round-the-door thatched cottage in deepest Dorset that had belonged to her grandparents and now, since their deaths, belonged to her.

In her grandparents' day it had been the only home she'd ever really had. With her parents in the armed forces, serving abroad, and herself packed off to boarding school at the age of eight, it had been her grandparents who had provided the home comforts and stability that her parents had not been in a position to provide. Now, determined to make it her own 'for ever' home, she was spending every penny she earned in undertaking the essential repairs and restoration that were required for such an old house—from a new thatched roof, to new drains…it all had to be done.

And now it nearly was. It only lacked a new kitchen and bathroom to replace the very ancient and decrepit units and sanitary ware and she could move in! All she needed was another ten thousand pounds to cover the cost.

That was why she was taking on all the modelling assignments she could—including this evening one now—squirrelling away every penny she could to get the cottage ready for moving in to.

She could hardly wait for that day. The glamour of being a fashion model had worn off long ago, and now it was only tiring and tedious. Besides, she had increasingly come to resent being constantly on show, all too often attracting the attention of men she had learned were only interested in her because she was a model.

She sheered her mind away from her thoughts. Jules had been a long time ago, and she was long over him. She'd been young and stupid and had believed that it was herself he'd cared for—when all along she'd simply been a trophy female to be wheeled out to impress his mates…

It had taught her a lesson though and had made her wary. She didn't want to be any man's trophy.

Her wariness gave her a degree of edginess towards men which she knew could put men off, however striking her looks. Sometimes she welcomed it. She wasn't one to put up with any hassle. Maybe something of her parents' emotional distance had rubbed off on her, she sometimes thought. They'd always taught her to stand up for herself, not to be cowed, overawed or over-impressed by anyone.

She certainly wasn't going to be overawed by the kind of people here tonight, knocking back champagne and snapping up couture clothes as if they were as cheap as chips! Just because they were stinking rich it didn't make them better than her in any way whatsoever—no way was anyone going to look down on her as some kind of walking clotheshorse!

Head held high, poker-faced, she kept on parading around, as she was being paid to do. The evening would end soon, and then she could clear off and get home.

Marc Derenz took a mouthful of champagne and shifted his weight restlessly, making some polite reply to whatever Hans Neuberger had just said to him. His mood was grim, and getting worse with every passing minute, but that was something he would never show to Hans.

A close friend of Marc's late father, Hans had been at his side during that bleak period after Marc's parents had been killed in a helicopter crash, when their only offspring had still been in his early twenties. It had been Hans who'd guided him through the complexities of mastering his formidable inheritance at so young an age.

Hans's business experience, as the owner of a major German engineering company, as well as his wisdom and kindness, were not things Marc would ever forget. He felt a bond of loyalty to the older man that was rare in his life, untrammelled by emotional ties as he had been since losing his parents.

It was a loyalty that was causing him problems right now, though. Only eighteen months ago Hans, then recently widowed following his wife's death from cancer, had been inveigled into a rash second marriage by a woman whom Marc had no hesitation in castigating as a gold-digger. And worse.

Celine Neuberger, here tonight to add to her already plentiful collection of couture gowns, had made no secret to Marc of the fact that she was finding her wealthy but middle-aged husband dull and uninteresting, now that she had him in her noose. And she had made no secret of the fact that she thought the opposite about Marc...

Marc's mouth tightened. Celine's eyes were hungry on him now, even though Marc was blanking her, but that did not seem to deter her. Had she been anyone other than Hans's wife Marc would have had no hesitation in ruthlessly sending her packing. It was a ruthlessness he'd had to learn early—first as heir to the Derenz billions, and then even more so after his parents' deaths.

Women were very, *very* keen on getting as close to those billions of his as possible. Ideally, by becoming Madame Marc Derenz.

Oh, at some point in his life, he acknowledged, there *would* be a Madame Derenz—when the time was right for him to marry and start a family. But she would be someone from the same wealthy background as himself.

It was advice his father had given him: to do what he himself had done. Marc's mother had been an heiress in her own right. And even for mere *affaires*, his father had warned him, it was best never to risk any liaison with anyone not from their own world of wealth and privilege. It was safer that way.

Mark knew the truth of it—only once had he made the mistake of ignoring his father's advice.

Celine Neuberger was addressing him now, her voice eager, and he was glad of the interruption to his thoughts. He had been recalling a time he did not care to remember, for he had been young and trusting then, and he had paid for that misplaced trust with a heartache he never wanted to experience again.

But what Celine had to say only worsened his mood sharply.

'Marc, have I told you that Hans has promised to buy a villa on the Côte d'Azur! And I've had the most *wonderful* idea!'

Celine's gushing voice grated on him.

'We could house-hunt from *your* gorgeous, gorgeous villa on Cap Pierre! *Do* say yes!'

Every instinct in Marc rebelled at the prospect,

but he was being put on the spot. In his parents' time Hans and his first wife had often been guests at the Villa Derenz—convivial occasions when the young Marc had had the company of Hans's son, Bernhardt, and had made enthusiastic use of the pool and gone sea bathing off the rocky shoreline of Cap Pierre. Good memories...

Marc felt a pang of nostalgic loss for those carefree days. Now, all he could say, resignedly, and with a forced smile, was, '*Bien sûr!* That would be delightful.' He tried to make the lie convincing. 'Delightful' was the last word to describe spending more time with Celine making eyes at him. Having to hold her at bay.

A triumphant Celine now pushed even further in a direction Marc had no intention of letting her advance. She turned to her husband. 'Darling, don't feel you have to stay any longer—Marc can see me back to our hotel.'

Hans turned to Marc, a grateful expression on his face. 'That would be so kind of you, Marc. I have to phone Bernhardt—matters to do with the forthcoming board meeting.'

Again, how could Marc object without giving Hans the reason?

The moment Hans had left Celine was, predictably, off the leash. 'Now, tell me,' she gushed, smiling warmly up at him, 'which would suit me best?' She gestured at the perambulating models.

Marc, knowing his mood was worsening with every passing moment in this impossible situation he'd been dumped in, lanced his gaze around to find the nearest model, whatever she was wearing, determined to give Celine the least opportunity for lingering.

But, as he did so, suddenly all thoughts of Celine went right out of his head.

During the fashion show itself he'd paid no attention to the endless parade of females striding up and down the catwalk, focussing instead on his phone. So now, as his eyes caught the figure of the model closest to where they stood, he felt his gaze riveted.

Tall, ultra-slender—yes. But then all the models were like that. None like this one, though, with rich chestnut hair glinting auburn, loosely pinned into an uplift that exposed a face he simply could not take his eyes from.

The perfect profile—and then, as she turned to change direction, he saw a strikingly beautiful face with sculpted cheekbones, magnificent eyes shot with sea-green, and a wide, lush mouth that was, at this moment, tight-set. The expression on her amazing face was professionally blank, but as his eyes focussed on her he felt his male antennae react instinctively—and on every frequency. She was quite incredible.

Without conscious volition he raised his free hand, summoning her over. For a second he thought she had not seen his gesture, for she was moving as if to keep stalking around as the rest of the models were doing. Then, tensing, she strode towards him. He could not take his eyes from her...

The thoughts in his head were flashing wildly. OK, so she was a model—and that put her out of reach from the off, because models were nearly always *not* from the kind of privileged background he insisted that any woman he showed interest in be from. But this one…

Whatever she had—and he was still analysing it, with his male antennae registering her on every frequency—it was making it dangerously hard for him to remember the rules of engagement he lived by.

As she approached, the impact she was making on him strengthened like a magnet drawing tempered steel. *Dieu*, but she was stunning! And now she was standing in front of him, a bare metre or so away.

He scrutinised her shamelessly, taking in her breathtaking beauty. And then he caught a flash in her eyes—as if she resented his scrutiny.

His own eyes narrowed reactively—what was her problem? She was a model; she was being paid to be looked at in the clothes she was wearing. OK, so in fact she might have been wearing a sack, for all he cared—it was her amazing beauty that was drawing his attention, not her gown.

But, abruptly, he veiled his appreciative scrutiny. It didn't matter how stunningly beautiful she was. He had not summoned her for any reason other than the one he gave voice to now. The *only* reason he would show any interest in her.

'So, what about this one?'

He turned to Celine. The sooner he could get the wretched woman to spend Hans's money on a gown—

any gown!—the sooner he would be able to get her
back to her hotel and finally be done with her for the
evening.

His eyes went back to the model. The number she
was wearing was purple—a kind of dark grape—in
raw silk, draped over her slight breasts, slithering
down her slender body. Again Marc felt that unstoppable reaction to her spectacular beauty. Again he did
his best to stop it—and again he failed.

'Hmm…' said Celine doubtfully. 'The colour is
too sombre for me, Marc. No.' She waved the model
away, dismissing her.

But Marc stayed her. 'Please turn around,' he instructed. The gown was a masterpiece—as was she—
and he wanted to see what she looked like from the
back.

The flash in those blue-green eyes came again,
and again Marc wondered at it as she executed a single revolution, revealing how the gown was almost
backless, exposing the sculpted contours of her spine,
the superb sheen of her pale skin. And as she came
back to face them he saw an expression of what could
only be hostility.

What is it with her? he found himself thinking.
Annoyance flickered through him. Why that reaction? It wasn't one he was used to when he paid attention to a woman—in his long experience women
wanted to draw his attention to them! His problem
was keeping women away from him, and without
vanity he knew that it was not only his wealth that
lured them. Nature had bestowed upon him gifts that

money could not buy—a six-foot-plus frame, and looks that usually had a powerful impact on women.

But not on this one, it seemed, and he felt that flicker of annoyance again as his gaze rested on her professionally blank face once more.

For a second—a fraction of a second—he thought he saw something behind that professional blankness. Something that was not that hostile flash either...

But then it was gone, and Celine was saying pettishly, 'Marc, *cherie*, I really don't like it.'

She waved the model away again, and she strode off with quickened stride, her body stiff. Marc's eyes followed her, unwilling to lose her in the throng which swallowed her up.

A pity she was a model...

For all her amazing looks, which were capable of piercing the black mood possessing him at having been landed with Hans's wretched adultery-minded wife, the stunning, flashing-eyed beauty was not someone, he knew perfectly well, he should allow himself to pursue...

She isn't from my world—let her go.

But a single word echoed in his head, all the same. *Domage...*

A pity...

Tara wheeled away, gaining the far side of the room as fast as she could. Her heart-rate was up and she knew why. Oh, she *knew* why!

She shut her eyes, wanting to blank the room. To blank the oh-so-conflicting reactions battling inside her head right now. She could feel them still, behind her closed eyes, slashing away at each other, fighting for supremacy.

Two overpowering emotions.

Impossible to tell which was uppermost!

The first—that instinctive, breath-catching one—had come the moment she'd seen that man looking at her...seen him for the first time. She certainly hadn't seen him at the fashion show, but then she never looked at the audience when she was on the catwalk. If she had—oh, she'd have remembered him all right...

No man had ever impacted on her as powerfully—as instantly. Talk about tall, dark and devastating! Sable-hair, cut short, a hard, tough-looking face with a blade of a nose, a strong jaw, a mouth set in a tight line. And eyes that could strip paint.

Or that could rest on her with a look in them that told her that he liked what he was seeing...

She felt a kind of electricity flicker through her and her expression darkened abruptly. The complete opposite emotion was scything through her head, cutting off the electricity.

Liked it so much he just saw fit to click his fingers and summon me over so he could inspect me!

She fought for reason. OK, so he hadn't actually clicked his fingers—but that imperious beckoning of his had been just as bad! Just as bad as the way he'd so blatantly looked her over...

And it wasn't the damn gown he was interested in.

That opposite emotion, with a jacking up of its voltage, shot through her again. As if she was once again feeling the impact of that dark, assessing inspection...

She threw the switch once more. *No—stop this, right now!* she told herself. So what if he'd put her back up? Why should she care? That over-made-up blonde he'd been with had treated her just as offhandedly, waving her away. So why get uptight about the man doing so?

And so what, she added for good measure, that she'd had that ridiculously OTT reaction to the man's physical impact on her? He and Blondie came from a world she wasn't part of and only ever saw from the outside—like at this private fashion show. Speaking of which...

She gave herself a mental shake, opened her eyes and continued with her blank-faced perambulations, showing off a gown she could never in all her life afford herself. She was here to work, to earn money, and she'd better get on with it.

Oh, and if she could to stay on this far side of the room... Well away from the source of those emotions in her head.

'Marc, *cherie*, now, *this* one is ideal! Don't you think?'

Celine's voice was a purr, but it grated on Marc like nails on a blackboard. However, at last, it seemed, Hans's wife had found a gown she liked and was stroking the gold satin material lovingly, not even looking at the model wearing it. This model was smiling hopefully at Marc, but he ignored her. He was not the slightest bit interested.

Not like that other one.

He cut his inappropriate thoughts off. Focussed on the problem at hand. How to divest himself of Hans's wife at last.

'Perfect!' he agreed, with relief in his voice. *Could they finally get out of here?*

His relief proved short-lived. Celine's scarlet-tipped fingers curled possessively around his arm.

'I've seen all I want here. I'll arrange a fitting for that gold dress while Hans and I are in London. But right now...' she smiled winningly at Marc '...do be an angel and take me to dinner! We could go to a club afterwards!'

Marc cut short her attempts to commandeer him for the rest of the evening. Never one to suffer irritation gladly, he knew his temper had been on a shortening fuse all evening. It was galling to see his father's old friend in the clutches of this appalling woman. How on earth could Hans not have seen through her?

But then dark memory came, though he wished it would not. Hadn't *he* been similarly blinded once himself?

Oh, he could tell himself he'd been young, and naïve, and far too trusting, but he'd been made a fool of all the same! Marianne had strung him along, playing on his youthful adoration of her, carefully cultivating his devotion to her—a devotion that had exploded in an instant.

Walking into that restaurant in Lyons, Marianne thinking I was still in Paris, seeing her there—

With another man. Older than Marc's barely two and twenty. Older and far wealthier.

Marc's father had still been alive then, and Marc only the prospective heir to the Derenz fortune. The man Marianne had been all over, cooing at, had been in his forties, and richer even than Marc's father. Marc had stared, the blood draining from his face, and had felt something dying inside him.

Then Marianne had seen him, and instead of trying to make any apology to him she had simply lifted her glass of champagne, tilted it mockingly at Marc, so the light would catch the huge diamond on her finger.

Shortly afterwards she had become the third wife of the man she'd been dining with. And Marc had learnt a lesson he had never, never forgotten.

Now, his tone terse, he spoke bluntly. 'Celine, I already have a dinner engagement tonight.'

Hans's wife was undeterred. 'Oh, if it's business I'll be good as gold,' she assured him airily, not relinquishing her hold on his arm. 'I sit through enough of Hans's deadly dull dinner meetings to know how!' she added waspishly. 'And we could still go clubbing afterwards…'

Marc shook his head. Time to stop Celine in her tracks. 'No, it's *not* business,' he told her, making the implication clear.

Celine's eyes narrowed. 'You're not seeing anyone at the moment. I know that,' she began, 'because I'd have heard about it otherwise.'

'And I'm sure you will,' Marc replied, jaw set.

He did *not* want a debate over this. He just wanted to get Celine off his hands before his temper reached snapping point.

'Well, who is it?' Celine demanded.

Marc felt his already short fuse shortening even more. He wanted to get out of here—now—and get shot of Celine. Any way he could. The fastest way he could.

He said the first thing that came into his head in this infuriating and wretched situation. 'One of the models here,' he answered tersely.

'Models?'

She said the word as if he'd said *waitresses* or *cleaners*. In Celine's eyes women who weren't rich— or weren't married to rich men—simply didn't exist. Let alone women who might possibly interest the likes of Marc Derenz.

Her eyes flashed petulantly. 'Well, which one, then?' she demanded. She was thwarted, and she was challenging him.

It was a challenge he could not help but meet— and he called her bluff with the first words that came into his head. 'The one in the dress you didn't like—'

'Her? But she looked right through you!' Celine exclaimed.

'She's not supposed to fraternise while she's working.'

Even as he spoke he was cursing himself. Why the hell had he said it was *that* model? The one who had stiffened up like a poker?

But he knew why. Because he was still trying to

put her out of his head, that was why—trying and fail-
ing. He'd been conscious of his eyes sifting through
the crowded room even as Celine was cooing over the
gown she was selecting, idly searching for the model
again. Irritated both that he was doing so and that he
could not see her.

She was keeping to the far side of the room. Not
coming anywhere near his eyeline again.

Because she is avoiding me?

The thought was in his head, bringing with it emotions that were at war with each other. He shouldn't
damn well be interested in her in the first place! For
all the reasons he always stuck to in his life. But he
could remind himself of those reasons all he liked—
he still wanted to catch another glimpse of her.

More than a glimpse.

Another thought flickered. Was it because she
hadn't immediately—eagerly!—returned his clear
look of interest in her that she was occupying his
thoughts like this? Had that intrigued him as well as
surprised him?

He didn't have time to think further, for Celine
was counter-calling *his* bluff.

'Well, *do* introduce me, *cherie*!' she challenged.

It was clear she didn't believe him, and Marc's
mouth tightened. He was not about to be outmanoeu-
vred by Hans's scheming wife. Nor was he going to
spend a minute longer in her company.

With a smile that strained his jaw, he murmured,
'Of course! One moment.' And he strode away across
the room with one purpose only, his mood grimmer

than ever. Whatever it took to shed the clinging Celine, he'd do it!

His eyes sliced through the throng, incisively seeking his target. And there she was. He felt the same kick go through him as had when he'd first summoned her across to him. That racehorse grace, that perfect profile—and those blue-green eyes which now, as he accosted her, were suddenly on him. And immediately, instantly blank.

And not in the least friendly.

Marc didn't give a damn—not now. His temper was at snapping point after what he'd put up with all evening.

He stood in front of her, blocking Celine's view of her from the other side of the room. Without preamble, he cut to the chase. Whether this was a moment of insanely stupid impulse, or the way out of a hole, he just did not care.

'How would you like,' he said to the model who was now staring at him with a closed, stony look on her stunningly beautiful face, 'to make five hundred pounds tonight?'

CHAPTER TWO

TARA HEARD THE WORDS, but they took a moment to register. She knew only that they'd been spoken with the slightest trace of an accent that she hadn't noticed in his curt instruction to her before.

She had still been trying to quench her reaction to the man who had just appeared out of nowhere in front of her. Blocking her. Demanding her attention. Just as he'd demanded she walk across to him and Blondie and twirl at his command.

OK, so that was her job here tonight, but it was the *way* he'd done it that had put her back up!

As now he was doing all over again—and worse. Because she did not *want* to feel that kick of high voltage again, that unwelcome quickening of her pulse as her eyes focussed, however determinedly she tried to resist, on that planed hard face and the dark eyes that were like cut obsidian.

The sense of what he'd just said belatedly reached her brain, as insulting as it was offensive.

She started to open her mouth, to skewer him with her reply—no *way* was she going to tolerate such an approach, whoever the hell this man was!—but he was speaking again. An irritated expression flashed across his face.

'Do *not*,' she heard him say, and there was a distinct tinge of boredom in his voice, as well as curt irritation, 'jump to the tediously predictable assumption you are clearly about to make. All I require is this. That you accompany myself and my guest back to her hotel, where—' he held up a silencing hand as Tara's mind raced ahead to envisage unspeakable debaucheries '—she will get out and you will stay in the car with me and then return here.'

The words were clipped from him, and then his eyes were going past her towards one of the fashion designer's hovering aides. He summoned him over with the same imperious gesture he'd used to draw her over to show off the gown she was wearing.

The man came scuttling forward. 'Monsieur Derenz, is there anything you require?' he asked eagerly.

Tara heard the obsequiousness in the man's voice and deplored it. The last thing rich guys like this one needed—let alone those with the kind of tough-looking face that he had, who expected everyone to jump at their bidding—was anyone kow-towing to them. It only encouraged them.

'Yes,' came the curt reply. 'I'd like to borrow your model for a very temporary engagement. I require a chaperone for my guest, Mrs Neuberger, as I escort her to her hotel. Your model will be away for no more than half an hour. Obviously I'll pay you for her time and take full financial liability for her gown. I take it there'll be no problem?'

The last was not a question—it was a statement. The aide nodded immediately. 'Of course, Monsieur Derenz.' His eyes snapped to Tara. 'Well? Don't just stand there! Monsieur Derenz is waiting!'

And that was that.

Fulminating, Tara knew she didn't have a choice. She needed the money. If she kicked off and refused then her agency would be told, and as this particular fashion designer was highly influential, there would be no hope that her objection to being shanghaied in this manner would be upheld.

All the same, she glared at the man shanghaiing her as the aide scuttled off again. 'What *is* this?' she demanded.

The man—this Monsieur Derenz, whoever he was, she thought tautly—looked at her impatiently. She'd never heard of him, and all the name did was confirm that he was not British—a deduction that went not just with his name and slight accent, but also with the air of Continental style that added something to his stance, and to the way he wore the clearly hand-made tuxedo that moulded his powerful frame in ways she knew she must not pay any attention to…

'You heard me—my guest needs a chaperone. And so do I!'

Tara could see his irritation deepen as he spoke.

'I want you to behave as if you know me. As if —' his mouth set '—we are having an affair.'

This time Tara did explode. *'What?'*

That dark flash of impatient irritation seared across his face again. 'Cool it,' he said tersely. 'I merely need my guest to be…disabused…of any expectations she may have of me.'

'She'd be welcome to you!' Tara muttered, hardly bothering to be inaudible.

How had she managed to get inveigled into this? Then something pinged back into her mind.

'Did you say five hundred pounds?' she demanded. No way was she going to come out of this empty-handed—not for putting up with this man commandeering her like this.

'Yes,' came the indifferent reply. 'Providing you don't waste any more of my time than this is already taking.'

Without waiting, he helped himself to her arm and started to walk back with her across the room, to where Tara could see the blonde woman who, apparently, had the idiotic idea that this man being tall, dark, handsome—and presumably, judging by how obsequious the aide had been, very rich—in any way compensated for his high-handed behaviour and peremptory manner.

As he walked her towards the unwanted blonde he bent his head to her. 'We have been together only a short while…you are reluctant to leave your work early, being highly conscientious—and if you pull away from me like that one more time your money is halved. Do you understand me?'

There was a grim note in his voice that put Tara's back up even more. But he was still talking.

'Now, tell me your name.'

It was another of those orders he clearly liked giving.

'Tara,' she said tightly. 'Tara Mackenzie. And I need to get my bag and coat first—'

'Unnecessary.' He cut her off. 'You'll be back here soon enough.'

They had reached the blonde, who was looking, Tara could see, like curdled milk at their approach.

'Ah, Celine—this is Tara. Tara—Frau Neuberger.'

His voice was more fulsome, and there might well be relief in it, Tara thought.

'Tara's been given the all-clear to leave early, so we can drop you off at your hotel. *Alors, allons-y.*'

He cupped a hand around Celine's elbow and drew them both forward simultaneously, his guiding grip allowing no delay. Moments later they were on the pavement outside the hotel, and Tara found herself stepping into a swish chauffeured limo. She settled herself carefully, mindful of her horrendously expensive gown, arranging the skirts so they did not crush.

The man she was supposed to be giving the impression that she was having an affair with—however absurd!—sat himself down heavily between her and the blonde—who, Tara was acidly amused to see, was faffing about with her seatbelt in order to get the man she wanted to make some form of body contact and fasten it for her. Sadly for her, it seemed he did not return the desire.

'Marc, *cherie*, thank you!' Tara heard the woman gush.

OK, Tara connected, Marc Derenz. She still had no

idea who he might be, but then so many of the richest of the rich were completely unknown to the wider world. To the plebs in it like herself. Well, what did it matter *who* he was? Nor did it matter that he seemed to possess the kind of physical appeal that was so annoyingly able to compete with her resistance to his peremptory and quite frankly dislikeable personality.

She glanced at him now, as the car moved off into the London evening traffic. His profile was just as tough-looking as his face—and the clear set of his jaw indicated that his mood had not improved in the slightest. She heard him make some terse reply in German to the blonde at his side, and then suddenly he was turning to Tara.

Something flickered in his eyes. Something that made Tara's insides go gulp even though she didn't want them to. Suddenly, out of nowhere, she felt the close physical proximity of this man—felt, of all things, that it wasn't Blondie who needed a chaperone, it was *her*…

That flicker in those dark, dark eyes came again. And this time it was more than just a flicker. It was a glint. A glint that went with the set of that tough jawline.

'Tara, *mon ange*—your seatbelt…'

His voice was a low murmur, nothing like as brusque as it had been when he'd spoken to Blondie, and there was only one word for its tone.

Intimate…

Out of nowhere, Tara felt herself catch her breath. She heard her thoughts scramble in her brain. *Oh, dear God, don't look at me like that! Don't speak to me like that! Because if you do...*

But there was something that was even more of an ordeal for her than the husky, intimate tone of his accented voice that was doing things to her that she did not want them to do—because the only reason she was here in this plush limo was to provide fleeting cover in a situation that was none of her making and that would be over and done with inside half an hour, tops...

Only it seemed that Marc Derenz was utterly oblivious to what she didn't want him to do to her—to the effect he was having on her that she *must* not let him see! Because her reaction to him was totally irrelevant! Totally and absolutely nothing to do with her real life. And totally at odds with the way she *should* think of him—as nothing but a rich man moving other people around for his own convenience and not even bothering to be polite about it!

But it was impossible to remember that as he leant across her, reaching for her seatbelt, invading her body space just as he invaded her senses. She could feel the hardness of his chest wall against her arm, see the cords of his strong neck, the sable feathering of his hair, the hard-edged jawline and the incised lines around his mouth. She could catch the expensive masculine scent of his aftershave. His own masculine scent...

Then, in a swift, assured movement, he was reaching for the seatbelt and pulling it across her. And in those few brief seconds the breath stopped in her lungs.

Oh, God, what has he got—what has he got?

But it was a futile question. She knew exactly what he had.

Raw, overpowering sexuality. Effortless, unconscious, and knocking her for six.

It was all over in a moment and he was back in his position in the middle of the wide, capacious seat, turning his attention to Blondie, who was relentlessly talking away to him in rapid French. Tara could see her long red nails pressed over Marc Derenz's sleeve, her face upturned to his—claiming his attention. Ignoring Tara.

The woman's rudeness started to annoy her—adding to her resentment of the way she'd been commandeered for this uninvited role. Well, if she was supposed to be riding shotgun, she had better behave as if she were!

Cutting right across Blondie's voluble chatter, she deliberately brushed her hand down Marc Derenz's sleeve. It was an effort to do so, but she forced herself. She had to recover from her ludicrous reaction to his fastening her seatbelt for her. She had to recover from her ludicrous reaction to his overpowering masculinity full-stop.

After all, she told herself robustly, she'd lived with her looks all her life and had been a model for years—she was a hardened operator, able to give short shrift to men importuning her. No way was this guy going to cow her just because he had the looks to melt her bones. No, it was time to prove to herself—and, damn it, to him too!—that she wasn't just going to meekly and mildly put up and shut up. Whatever it was about him that riled her so, she wasn't going to let him call all the shots.

In which case…

'Marc, baby, I'm sorry I gave you a hard time over leaving early. Forgive me?' She leant into him just a fraction, quite deliberately, and put a husky, cajoling note into her voice.

His head swivelled. For a moment she saw an expression in his eyes that should have been a warning to her. But it was too late to regret drawing his attention to her.

'You'll have to accept, *mon ange*, that I have severe time constraints in my life. *Hélas*, I have to be in Geneva tomorrow, so I wanted to make the most of tonight.'

He sounded regretful. And intimate. It was an intimacy that curled right down her body. He didn't have a strong French accent, but, boy, what he had worked…

And then Blondie was jabbering in German, and he turned to her to reply.

Relief drenched through Tara. If that was him simply *acting* the role of attentive lover…

She dragged her mind away, steadied her breathing. Oh, sweet Lord, whatever he had, he definitely had what it took to get past her defences.

Her expression changed. It was just as well that his personality didn't match his looks—he had all the winning charm of a ten-ton boulder, crushing everyone around him! And it was even more just as well, she was honest enough to admit, that her acquaintance with this man was going to be extremely short-lived.

She'd see this exercise through, get back to work, and be a useful five hundred pounds the richer for it. All feeding into the Escape to My Cottage in the Country fund. She made herself focus on that subject for the remainder of the thankfully short journey, doing her best to ignore the very difficult to ignore presence of the man sitting next to her, and grateful that he was being monopolised by Blondie, who was clearly making the most of him.

As the car pulled up under the portico of the woman's hotel Tara sat meekly while the other two got out. Marc Derenz escorted Blondie indoors, to emerge some minutes later and throw himself back into the car, this time on the far side vacated by Blondie.

'Thank God!' Tara heard him say—and he sounded as if he meant it.

Tara couldn't resist. He was such a charmless specimen, however ludicrously good-looking. 'Such a bore, aren't they?' she said sweetly. 'Women who don't get the message.'

Dark eyes immediately swivelled to her, and Tara reeled inwardly with the impact. It was like being seared by a laser set to stun. Despite the effort it cost her, she gritted her teeth, refusing to blink or back down.

He didn't deign to answer, merely flicked out his phone and jabbed at it. A moment later he was in full flood to someone he clearly wanted to talk to—unlike herself—and Tara assumed from his businesslike tone, that business was what it was.

She leant back, not sure if she was feeling irritated by his manner or just glad the whole escapade was almost over. Even so, she unconsciously felt her head twist slightly as the car moved back out into the traffic, so she could behold his profile. Again, she felt that annoyingly vulnerable reaction to him, that skip in her pulse. She jerked her head away.

Oh, damn the man! He might radiate raw sexuality on every wavelength, but his granite personality was a total turn-off. The minute she was out of here and had the money he'd promised her she would never think about him again.

Five minutes later they were back at the hotel where the fashion show was being held and she was climbing out of the limo. Pointedly, she held her door open—no way was he driving off without paying her.

'You said five hundred,' she said, holding out her hand expectantly. The only reason, she reminded herself grimly, that she had anything to do with this man was for money! No other reason.

For a moment he just looked at her, his face closed. Then he got out of the car, standing in front of her. He was taller than her, even with her high heels, and it wasn't something she was accustomed to in men.

She felt her jaw set. There was something about the way he was looking at her. As if he were considering something. She lifted her chin that much higher, eyeballing him, hand still outstretched for her pay-off.

His dark eyes were veiled, unreadable.

'My money, please,' she said crisply. What was going on? Was he going to try and welch on the deal? For a sum that would be utterly trivial to a man like him?

Then, abruptly, she realised why he was not reaching for his wallet. Because he was reaching for her hand.

Before she could stop him, or step away, he'd taken hold of it and was raising it to his mouth. His expression as he did so had changed. Changed devastatingly.

Tara felt her lungs seize—felt everything seize.

Oh, God, she heard her inner voice say, silently and faintly and with absolute dismay, *don't do this to me...*

But it was too late. With a glint in his obsidian eyes, as if he knew perfectly well that what he was doing would sideswipe her totally, he turned her hand over in his, exposing the tender skin of her wrist.

Eyelashes far too long for a man with a face that tough swept down, veiling those dark, mordant eyes of his. And then his mouth, like silken velvet, was brushing that oh-so-delicate skin, gliding across it with deliberate slowness. Soft, sensuous, devastating.

She felt her eyelids flutter shut, felt a ludicrous weakness flood her body. Desperately she tried to negate it. It was just skin touching skin! But her attempt to reduce it to such banality was futile. Totally futile. The warm, grazing caress of his mouth on the sensitive surface of her skin focussed every nerve-ending in her entire body just on her wrist. She was melting, dissolving...

He dropped her hand, straightened. 'Thank you,' he murmured, his voice low, his eyes holding hers.

The darkling glint in them was still there, but there was something more to it—something that kept her lungs immobile. 'Thank you for your co-operation this evening.'

There was the merest hint of amusement in his voice. She snatched her hand away, as if it had been touched by a red-hot bar of iron, not by the sensuous, seductive glide of his mouth.

She had to recover—any way she could. 'I only did it for the money!' she gritted, going back to eyeballing him, defying him to think otherwise.

She saw his expression harden. Close. Whatever had been there, even if only to taunt her, had vanished. Now there was only the personality of that crushing boulder back in evidence.

With a clearly deliberate gesture he reached for his wallet in the inner pocket of his tailored dinner jacket, and an equally deliberately flicked it open. Stone-faced—determinedly so—Tara watched him peel off the requisite number of fifty-pound notes and hold them out to her.

She took them from him, her colour heightened. There was something about standing here and having a man handing her money—any man, let alone this damn one!

He was looking at her with that deliberately impassive expression on his face, but there was something in the depths of those dark veiled eyes of his that made her react on total impulse. The man was so totally charmless, so totally forbidding, and yet he had so *totally* shot to pieces her usual cool-as-ice reac-

tion to any kind of physical contact with a man. She'd
let him do all that wrist-kissing, *let* him taunt her as
he had and hadn't even *tried* to pull away from him.

Now, in an overpowering impulse to get some kind
of retaliation, she lifted the topmost fifty-pound note
from the wad in her hand. Stepping forward, she gave
her saccharine smile again and with deliberate inso-
lence tucked the fifty-pound note into his front jacket
pocket and patted it.

'Buy yourself a drink, Mr Derenz,' she told him
sweetly. 'You look like you could use one!'

She turned on her high heel, stalking away back
into the hotel, not caring about his reaction. If she
never saw Marc Derenz again it would be too soon!
A man like him could only be bad, bad news.

A man who, like no other man she'd ever met,
could turn her into melting ice-cream with a taunting
wrist-kiss and a veiled glance from those dark eyes—
and who could equally swiftly make her mad as fire
with his imperious manner and rock-like personality.

Yes, she thought darkly, *definitely* bad news.

On *so* many counts.

Behind her, stock-still on the pavement, knowing the
doorman had been covertly observing the exchange
and not giving a damn, Marc watched her disappear
from sight, the skirts of her gown billowing around
her long, long legs, that glorious chestnut hair catching the light. In his memory he could still taste the
silken scent of the pale skin at her wrist, the warmth
of the pulse beneath the surface.

Then, his expression still mask-like, he turned away to climb back into his car, and be driven to his own hotel.

As if mentally rousing himself, he reached for the crumpled note in his breast pocket. He slipped it back into his wallet, depleted now of the four hundred and fifty pounds that were in her possession. As his wallet held his gaze, he felt as if the contents were reminding him of something important to him. That he would be wise not to forget.

How much he had wanted to silence that acidly saccharine mouth of hers, taunting him in a way that right now, in the mood he'd been in all evening, had *not* been wise at all... Silence it in the only way he wanted...

No. Tara Mackenzie was not for him—not on any terms. All his life he'd played the game of romance by the rules he'd set out for himself, to keep himself safe, and it was out of the question to consider breaking them. Not even for a woman like that.

After all, he mused, had it not been for the wretched Celine he would never even have encountered her. Now all he wanted was to put both of them behind him. For good.

It would be less than a fortnight later, however, that he would be forced to do neither. And it would blacken his mood to new depths of exasperatedly irate displeasure...

Tara was looking at kitchens and bathrooms online, trying to budget for the best bargains. However she calculated it, she still definitely needed at least another ten thousand pounds to get it all done. And even living in London as cheaply as she could—including staying in this run-down flat-share—it would take, she reckoned, a good six months to save that much.

What I need is some nice source of quick, easy dosh!

She gave a wry twist of a smile tinged with acerbity. Well, she'd made that five hundred pounds quickly enough—just for keeping the oh-so-charmless Marc Derenz safe from Blondie.

Memory swooped on her—that velvet touch of his mouth on the tender inside of her wrist...

A rasp of annoyance broke from her—with herself, for remembering it, for feeling that tremor that it had aroused go through her again now.

He only did it to taunt you! No other reason.

With an impatient resolve to put the wretched man out of her thoughts, she went back to her online perusal. Moving to Dorset—*that* was important to her. Not some obnoxious zillionaire who'd put her back up from the very first. Nor some man who could set her pulse racing...a man who was so, so wrong for her...

A thought sifted across her mind. Would there ever be a man who *was* right for her, though?

Yes, she thought determinedly—one day there *would* be. But she wasn't going to find him here in London, in her life as a model. No, it would be someone she'd meet when she'd started her new life in the country. Someone who didn't know her as a model at all, and who didn't see her as a trophy to show off with. Her thoughts ran on. Someone who was, oh, maybe a vet—or a farmer, even—at home in the countryside…

She pressed her lips together, giving a smothered snort. Well, one thing was for sure, it would not be Marc Derenz. And, anyway, she was never going to set eyes on him again.

A sharp rapping on the front door of the flat made her jump. She gave a sigh of irritation. Probably one of her flatmates had forgotten her keys.

She put her laptop aside, padded to the door, and opened it.

And stepped back in total shock.

It was the last person on earth she'd ever expected to see again.

Marc Derenz.

CHAPTER THREE

MARC'S MOOD WAS BLACK. Blacker even than it had been that torturous evening at the fashion show, with Celine trying to corner him. He'd hoped the brush-off he'd given her would mean she'd give up. He'd been wrong.

She was still plaguing him—still set on inviting herself to the Villa Derenz on the blatant pretext of house-hunting. It had been impossible to refuse Hans's apologetic request—and now he'd been landed with them arriving this week.

Marc's reaction had been instant—and implacable. He'd blocked her before—he would just have to do it again. However damn irritating it was to have to do so.

His eyes rested now on the means he was going to have to use. Tara Mackenzie.

He knew her name, and it had been easy enough to find out where she lived. He cast a disparaging eye around the dingy apartment. The front door opened on to the lounge, which was cheaply furnished and messy—belongings were scattered on battered settees, and a rack of washing was drying in front of the window.

His gaze swept round to the woman he'd tracked down.

And he veiled it immediately.

Even casually dressed, in jeans and a loose shirt, Tara Mackenzie was a complete knockout. Every bit as stunning as he remembered her. The same insistent, visceral response to her that he'd felt at that fashion show, that he'd been doing his damnedest to expel from his memory, flared in him again. Deplorable, but powerful. Far too powerful.

He crushed it down.

She was staring at him now, with those amazing blue-green eyes of hers, and had opened her mouth to speak. He pre-empted her. He wanted this sorted as swiftly as possible.

'I need to talk to you. I have a business proposition to put to you.'

His voice was clipped to the point of curtness. Just as it had been before at the fashion show. Tara's hackles rose automatically. She was still reeling from seeing him again—still reeling from the overpowering impact he was having on her, that seemed to be jacking up the voltage of her body's electricity as if she'd suddenly been plugged into the mains.

This time he was not in a hand-made tux, but in a dark grey killer business suit that screamed *Mr Rich and Powerful! Don't mess me about!*

Just as the look on his face did. That closed expression on his hard-planed, utterly unfairly devastating features and the obvious aura of impatience about him. His automatic expectation that she would meekly listen to whatever it was he was about to say.

He went on in the same curt, clipped voice, his faint accent almost totally supressed. 'Extend the role you adopted at the fashion show and you can make five thousand pounds out of it,' he said, not bothering with any preamble.

Tara frowned, and then she smiled, enlightenment dawning. It wasn't a genuine smile, but it helped her control that voltage hammering through her.

'Blondie still pestering you, is she?' she put to him.

She saw his expression tighten at her sardonic observation. Obviously he was annoyed, but he was acknowledging, tacitly, what she had said.

'Well?' It was his only response.

'Tell me more.' Tara smiled sweetly.

The electricity kindled by his utterly unexpected arrival had sparked a kind of exhilaration in her. It dawned on her that he was resenting having to approach her. And that, she knew, feeling another spark inside her, was really quite gratifying...

Just why that should be so she did not pause to examine.

He took a short breath, his eyes still like lasers on her. 'A week of your time—ten days at the most. It would be...residential,' he said, 'but entirely...' His eyes suddenly closed over their previous expression. 'Entirely synthetically so. In other words, on the same basis as before.' A tight, non-humorous smile tightened his mouth. 'For appearances only.'

Was there a warning in the way he'd said 'only'?

Tara didn't know and didn't care. It was entirely irrel-evant. Of course it was 'appearances only'. No other possibility. Any woman thinking anything more of him would need her head examined!

'You would,' he continued, in that businesslike voice, 'be my house guest.'

Tara's eyebrows rose. 'Along with Blondie, I take it?'

He gave a brief nod. 'Precisely so.'

'And I get to run interference?'

He nodded again, impatience visible in his man-ner but saying nothing, only letting those laser eyes of his rest on her, as if trying to bend her to his im-placable will.

And then suddenly, out of nowhere, there was some-thing in them that was a like a kick in her system—something that flashed like a warning light in her head…as if she stood upon the brink of a precipice she hadn't even realised was there.

Just as suddenly it was gone. Had she imagined it? That sudden change somewhere at the back of those unreadable slate-dark eyes? Something he'd swiftly blanked? She must have, she decided. There was nothing in his expression now but impatience. He wanted an answer. And fast.

But she did not like being hustled. She took a breath and met his eyes, though she was conscious of the way she'd crossed her arms firmly over her chest, as if keeping him and his imposing, utterly out of place presence at bay.

'OK, do I have this right? You will pay me five thousand pounds to spend up to ten days, max, as your house guest, and behave—strictly in public only—' she made sure she emphasised that part '—as if I am your current squeeze, just as I did on that limo ride the other night, while your *other* house guest— Blondie—gets the message that, sadly for her, you are not available for whatever adulterous purpose she would like you to be. Is that it?' She raised her eyebrows again questioningly.

His expression did not change. He merely inclined his sable-haired head minutely.

Tara thought about it. 'Half up front,' she said.

He didn't blink. 'No. You might not show up,' he said flatly.

His eyes flicked around their shabby surroundings and Tara got the message. Someone who had to live in a place like this might indeed walk off with two and a half thousand pounds.

She made herself look at him. The man was loaded. He had to be, the way he behaved, the lifestyle he had—chauffeur-driven limo, hanging around at couture fashion shows in swanky hotels. No way was she going to be short-changed by him. After all, pro rata, the five hundred pounds for the bare half-hour previously was *way* more generous than this offer.

'Ten thousand,' she said bluntly.

It would be chicken-feed to a man like him, but a huge sum for herself. And exactly what she needed for her cottage. For a moment she wondered if she'd overplayed her hand. But then, maybe she should be glad if she had. Could she *really* face spending any more time in the company of this man? The reasons not to were not just her resistance to his rock-like personality...

Caution started to backfill the ridiculously heady sense of sparking exhilaration she had felt. Caution that came too late.

The voltage in those eyes seared. Then abruptly cut out. 'OK. Ten thousand,' he gritted out. As if she'd just pulled a tooth from his steeled jaw.

That spark of exhilaration surged again inside her, overriding the vanished and defeated caution. Boy, was he mad she'd pushed the price up!

She felt herself smile—a genuine one this time. And then, abruptly, her triumph crashed. With a gesture that was vivid in her memory, he was coolly extracting his gold-monogrammed leather wallet from his jacket, peeling off a fifty-pound note. Then a second one.

Reaching forward, with a glint in his eye that gave her utterly insufficient warning, even though it should have, he tucked the two notes into the front pocket of the shirt she was wearing.

'A little something on account,' he said, and there was a purr in his voice that told her that this was exactly what she knew it was.

His comeback for her daring to tip him with his own money.

She opened her mouth to spit something at him but he was turning on his heel. Striding from the room. Informing her, as he rapidly took his leave, that arrangements would be made via her agency.

Then he was gone.

Taking a long, deliberate breath, she removed the

two fifty-pound notes from her breast pocket and stared at them. That, she reminded herself bluntly, was the nature of her relationship with Marc Derenz. And she had better not lose sight of it. The only reason he'd sought her out was to buy her time, because she could be useful to him. No other reason.

And I wouldn't want it to be for any other reason!

Her adjuration to herself was stern. Just why it was that Marc Derenz, of all the men she'd ever encountered in her life, could have this devastating effect on her, she didn't know. She knew only that no good could come of it. Her world was not his, and never would be.

It was hard to remember her warning to herself as, a week later, she turned to look out through the porthole of the plane heading for the Côte d'Azur. Their destination had been a little detail Marc Derenz had omitted to inform her of, but she had no complaint. Just the opposite. Her mood was soaring. To spend a whole week at least on the fabled French Riviera—and be paid for doing so! Life didn't get any better.

She didn't even care that she was being flown out Economy, in spite of how rich the man was. And, boy, was he *rich*! She'd looked him up—and her eyebrows had gone up as well.

Marc Derenz, Chairman of Banc Derenz. She'd never heard of it, but then, why would she have? It was headquartered in Paris, for a start, and it was not a bank for the likes of her, thank you very much! Oh, no, if you banked at Banc Derenz you were rich—

very, *very* rich. You had investment managers and fund managers and portfolio managers and high net worth individual account managers—all entirely at your disposal to ensure you got the very highest returns on your millions and zillions.

As for her destination—the Villa Derenz was featured in architectural journals and was apparently famous as being a perfect example of Art Deco style.

It was something she could agree with a few hours later, as she was conducted across a marble-floored hall and up a sweeping marble staircase like something out of a nineteen-thirties Hollywood movie.

She was shown into a bedroom, its décor pale grey and with silvered furniture. She looked about her appreciatively. This was *fabulous*. It was a sentiment she echoed when she walked out onto the balcony that ran the length of the frontage of the villa. Her breath caught, her eyes lighting up. Verdant green lawns surrounded the brilliant white building, pierced only by a turquoise circular pool and edged by greenery up to the rocky shoreline of the Cap. Beyond, the brilliant azure of the Mediterranean confirmed the name of this coastline.

She gazed with pleasure. No wonder the rich liked being rich if it got them a place like this.

And I get to stay here!

She went back inside to help the pair of maids unpacking her clothes. They weren't her own clothes— a stylist had selected them, on Marc Derenz's orders, Tara assumed, as being suitable for the role she was going to play. For all that, she would definitely enjoy wearing them. Actually wearing them for herself, not for other women to buy—it would be a novelty she would make the most of.

She would make the most of everything about her time here. Starting with relishing the delicious lunch about to be served to her out on the balcony, under a shady parasol, followed by a relaxing siesta on a conveniently placed sun lounger in the warm early summer sunshine.

Where Marc Derenz was she didn't know—presumably he'd turn up at some point and she would go on duty. Till then...

'Don't burn.'

The voice that woke Tara was deep and familiar, and its abrupt tone told her instantly that concern for her well-being was not behind the statement.

Her eyes flared open, and for a moment the tall figure of the man who was going to pay her ten thousand pounds for staying in his luxury villa in the South of France loomed darkly over her.

She levered herself up on her elbows. 'I've got sun cream on,' she replied.

'Yes, well, I don't want you looking like a boiled lobster,' Marc Derenz said disparagingly. 'And it's time for you to start work.'

She sat up straight, feeling her arms for the thin straps of her swimsuit, which she'd pushed down to avoid tan marks on her shoulders. As she did so she felt the suit dip dangerously low over her breasts. And she felt suddenly, out of nowhere, a burning consciousness of the fact that those hard, dark eyes were targeted on her, and that all that concealed her nakedness was a single piece of thin stretchy material.

Deliberately, she busied herself picking up her wrap, studiedly winding it around herself without looking at him. Whether he was looking at her still she did not care.

I'm going to have to get used to this—to the impact he has on me. And fast. I can't go on feeling so ridiculously self-conscious. I've got to learn to blank him.

With that instruction firmly in mind, she finished knotting her wrap securely and looked across at him. Against the sun he seemed even taller and darker. He was wearing another of his killer business suits, pale grey this time, with a sharp silk tie and what would obviously be twenty-four-carat gold cufflinks and tiepin.

Tara made herself look and sound equally businesslike. 'OK,' she said. 'What's the next thing on the agenda, then?'

'Your briefing,' Marc Derenz replied succinctly.

His pose altered slightly and he nodded his head at a chair by the table, seating himself on a second chair, crossing one perfectly creased trouser leg over the other.

'Right,' he started in a brisk voice as she sat where he'd bade her. 'There are some ground rules. This, Ms Mackenzie, is a *job*. Not a holiday.'

Marc rested his eyes on her impassively. But he was masking a distinctly less impassive emotion. Arriving here from Paris to find her sunning herself on the balcony had not impressed him. Or, to be precise, she had not impressed him with her lack of recognition that she was here to fulfil a contractual obligation. In every other respect he'd been very, *very* impressed…

Dieu, but she possessed a body! He'd known she did, but to see it displayed for him like that, before she'd become aware of his presence, had been a pleasure he had indulged in for longer than was prudent.

Because it didn't matter how spectacular her figure was, let alone her face, this was—as he was now reminding her so brusquely—a job, not a holiday.

Certainly not anything else.

His thoughts cut out like a guillotine slicing down. In the days since he had hired her to keep Celine Neuberger at bay he'd had plenty of second thoughts. And third thoughts. Had he been incredibly rash to bring her here? Was he playing with matches near gunpowder?

Seeing her again now, viewing that fantastic body of hers, seeing her stunning beauty right in front of him again, and not only in the memories he'd done his best to crush, was…*unsettling*.

Abruptly he reminded himself that she was not a woman from his world, but a woman he'd admitted into his life briefly, under duress only, and not by free choice. That that did not mean he could now break the rules of a lifetime—rules that had served him well ever since the youthful fiasco over Marianne that had cost him so dearly. Oh, not in money—in heartache that he never wanted to feel again.

But I was young then! A stripling! It was calf

love, nothing more than that, and that's why it hit me so hard.

Now he was a stripling no longer, but a seasoned man, in his thirties, sure of himself, and sure of what he wanted and how to get it. Sure of his relationships with the women he selected for his *amours*. Women who were nothing like the one now sitting opposite him, taking money for her time here.

That was what he must remember. *She* would— that was for certain. It was the reason she was here… the reason she'd accompanied him from the fashion show. She'd made it perfectly clear then—and again when she'd so brazenly upped what he'd been prepared to offer her to come out here now. That was warning enough, surely?

However stunning her face and figure—however powerful her appeal—his relationship with Tara Mackenzie must be strictly professional only. She was here, as he reminded himself yet again, only to do a job.

It was, therefore, in a brisk, businesslike tone that he continued now. 'The Neubergers are arriving this evening. From then on, until they leave, you will assume the role you are here to play. What is essential, however,' he went on, 'is that you understand you are here to *act* the part only. You are *not* to imagine we actually have a relationship of any kind whatsoever or that one is possible at all. Do you understand me?'

Tara felt herself bridling as his dark eyes bored into hers. He was doing it again! Putting her back *right* up. And not just in the way he'd said things—in *what* he had said.

Warning me off him. Telling me not to get ideas about him. Oh, thank you—yes, thank you so much, Monsieur Derenz. It was so necessary to warn me off you! Not.

Would she really ever consider a man with the personality of a lump of granite, who clearly thought every woman in the world was after him?

Indignation sparked furiously in her. 'Of course, Monsieur Derenz. I understand perfectly, Monsieur Derenz. Whatever you say, Monsieur Derenz,' Tara intoned fulsomely, venting her objection to his high-handed warning.

His eyes flashed darkly and his arched eyebrows snapped together in displeasure. 'Don't irritate me more than you already have, Ms Mackenzie,' he said witheringly.

'And don't *you*, Monsieur Derenz,' she shot back, bridling even more at his impatient put-down, 'entertain the totally unwarranted assumption that I have *any* desire to do anything more than *act* the part I am here to play! And,' she continued, refusing to be cowed by the increasingly black look on his face, 'I expect *you* to do likewise. There is to be *no* repeat of that little wrist-kissing stunt you pulled just before I went back into the fashion show!' She saw his expression stiffen and ploughed on. 'No unwarranted body contact at all. I appreciate that my role must be convincing—but it is for *public* view only.'

Even just *pretending* to be on intimate terms with

him was going to be a challenge. A challenge that, now she was seeing him again, was making a hollow form inside her. Oh, *what* did the wretched man have that got to her like this?

Deliberately, she made herself think not about how drop-dead devastating he was, sitting there in his killer suit, drawing her hapless gaze to his hard-featured face with the night-dark eyes, but of how obnoxious his manner was. Yes, that was a much safer way to think of him!

The best way of all, though, would be to do what he was doing, annoying though it was to admit it—treat this entire matter as simply a professional engagement.

So, with a deep breath, and a resumption of her cool tone, she asked in a no-nonsense, businesslike way, 'OK—so, the Neubergers… You'd better tell me what I'll be expected to know.'

He didn't seem to like it that she'd taken control of the conversation—but then, she thought acidly, Marc Derenz was clearly used to calling all the shots, all the time. Maybe his employees—and she was one herself, after all, however temporary—were not expected to speak before the august chairman of Banc Derenz.

However, he answered her readily enough, in a no-nonsense tone matching her own.

'Hans Neuberger is head of Neuberger Fabrik—a major German engineering company based in Frankfurt. He is a long-standing family friend and he knows this villa well from many previous visits. Celine is his second wife—Hans was a widower—and their mar-

riage is a relatively recent one…less than two years.
He has adult children from his first marriage—'

'Who hate Celine's guts,' put in Tara knowingly.

He made no reply, only continued as if she had not
spoken. 'Celine has persuaded her husband to house-
hunt for a villa here, and on that pretext she has invited herself to stay, with predictably obvious intent.'

His tone was icy and Tara found herself chilled
by it. Even more so as he continued in the same cold
voice.

'I will not conceal from you the fact that I consider Hans's marriage to Celine…ill-advised. The
woman targeted him for his wealth, and she presumes
to target myself—' his tone dropped from cold to
Arctic '—as a source of…*entertainment.*' His voice
plunged to absolute zero. 'This demonstrates just how
ill-advised their marriage is. Were Hans Neuberger
anything other than, as I have said, a long-standing
family friend, there would be absolutely no question.
I would have no hesitation in sending her packing.'

Tara took a slicing breath. 'No, no question at
all…' she muttered.

It was unnerving to see just how cold Marc Derenz
could be—and how ruthless. Imperious in manner, intemperate in mood—yes, she'd seen that already—but
this display of icy ruthlessness was something else…

He got to his feet. 'As it is, however, I am required,
for Hans's sake, to proceed by taking a more…*subtle*
approach.'

Tara gave a tight smile. 'To demonstrate to her that
the…*vacancy* in your life is fully occupied?'

His eyes rested on her, dark and unreadable. 'Precisely,' he said.

He got to his feet. He seemed taller than ever, looming over her. He glanced at his watch—doubtless one of those custom-made jobs, she assumed, that cost more than a house. Then his eyes flicked back to her. She got the feeling that he'd suddenly veiled them, and found herself doing likewise with her own. Instinctively she reached for her discarded sunglasses, as if for protection.

'Cocktails at eight, Ms Mackenzie. Do not be late. I don't appreciate tardiness,' he instructed brusquely.

With that, he left her. And as she watched him stride across the balcony Tara suddenly felt as if she'd gone six rounds with a heavyweight.

She picked up her book, conscious that her heart-rate was elevated. One thing was for sure—she was going to earn her money here.

As she settled back in her lounger a stray thought flickered. *I should have asked for danger money—I think I'm going to need it.*

But whether that would protect her from Marc Derenz's unyieldingly flinty manner, or from his much more devastating impact on her, she did not care to examine…

CHAPTER FOUR

Marc was in his office, staring moodily at his computer screen, paying the display no attention. He kept a fully kitted-out office in all his properties, so that he could keep constant tabs on his business affairs.

It had been his habit to do so ever since his vast inheritance had landed on his too-young shoulders. If he hadn't kept a tight grip on everything, shown everyone he was capable of running the bank, he'd have been sidelined by his own board. Doing so had made him appear hard-nosed, even arrogant sometimes, he was aware, but imposing his will on men a generation older than him had been essential. Even now, over a decade on, the habit of command was ingrained in him, whoever he was dealing with.

Including women who were being paid handsomely to do a very simple job, and yet who seemed to find it impossible not to simply take on board his very clear instructions without constantly answering him back!

His mouth tightened. This nonsense with Hans's wife was causing him quite enough grief as it was.

To have Tara Mackenzie constantly interrupting him, gainsaying him, answering him back, was just intolerable!

He gave a sigh of exasperation. She had better adopt a more gracious and compliant attitude once the Neubergers arrived, or she would never convince the wretched Celine that they were an item.

Why can't she just be like other women are with me? he demanded of himself in exasperation. All his life women had been eager to please him. So why was this one so damn *un*-eager? With her stunning looks, she could have made him far better disposed towards her.

Maybe I should win her over...

Whatever her self-righteous protestations, she had, he knew with his every well-honed male instinct, reacted just the way he'd intended when he'd kissed that tender spot inside her wrist that evening of the fashion show... It had had exactly the effect on her he'd wanted. Started to melt her...

So maybe I should do more of that, not less...

The thought played in his mind. It was tempting... oh, so tempting...to turn that obstreperous antagonism towards him to something much more...*co-operative*...

It would be a challenge, certainly—he had no doubt of that. But maybe he would welcome such a challenge. It would be an intriguing novelty, after all. So different from being besieged by over-eager females...

He thrust the thought from him, steeling his jaw. No, that would *not* be a good idea! Did he *really* have to run through all the reasons why Tara Mackenzie, whatever her allure, was out of bounds to him?

No, he did not. He pulled his keyboard decisively towards him. All he had to do was get through this coming week, using the woman he was paying an exorbitant amount of money, to keep the wretched Celine off his case.

Tara Mackenzie was here to do a job, and then leave. That was all.

All.

Decision reaffirmed, he went back to his work.

Tara cast a professionally critical eye over her reflection. And *professional* was the word she had to keep uppermost in her mind. This, she reminded herself sternly, was just as much a job as striding down a catwalk. And Marc Derenz was simply her employer. She frowned momentarily. Thankfully only for a week or so.

For a week I can put up with his overbearing manner!

And, of course, for the ten thousand pounds he was paying her.

She nodded at her reflection, that showed her in a knee-length royal blue cocktail dress, from a very exclusive luxury label, her make-up immaculate, hair in a French pleat, and one of the pieces of top-brand costume jewellery she'd found in the suitcases around her neck. Yes, she looked the part—the latest woman in Marc Derenz's life. Couture-dressed and expensive.

So—time to go onstage. One of the maids had told

her she was being waited for downstairs, so she made her way to the head of the Hollywood-style staircase. From the top she could see a white-jacketed staff member opening the huge front doors and stepping aside to let Marc Derenz's guests enter, just as Marc himself issued forth from another ground-floor room.

And stopped dead.

Immediately Tara could see why. This was not the Neubergers arriving—this was Frau Neuberger *toute seule.*

Celine—*sans mari*—was dressed to kill in a tailored silk suit in crème-de-menthe, five-inch heels, and a handbag that Tara knew, from her modelling expertise, had a waiting list of over a year and wouldn't give you change from twenty thousand pounds…

'Marc, *cherie*!' Celine cooed as she came up to her host, who was still standing frozen, and lavished air kisses upon him. 'How *wonderful* to be here!'

'Where is Hans?' Tara heard him ask bluntly, at which Celine gave an airy wave.

'Oh, I told him we had no need of him! We'll do *perfectly* well on our own!' She patted Marc's cheek insouciantly with her bare hand, lingering over the contact with her varnished fingernails.

Tara wanted to laugh. Celine was in high fettle, despite the thunderous expression on her quarry's face. Well, time to disabuse her of her hopes.

She started forward, heels tapping on the marble stairs. A wide, welcoming smile parted her lips. 'Celine, how lovely to meet you again!' she exclaimed. 'We're so glad you were able to come!'

She reached the hallway, marshalling herself alongside Marc Derenz. Her pulse was not entirely steady—and that was nothing to do with Celine Neuberger and everything to do with the way Marc Derenz had looked at her as she'd walked down towards them. The way his hard dark eyes had focussed totally on her, as if pinning her with his gaze. A gaze that this time was not like a laser, but more... Appreciative. Liking what it saw. More than liking...

She felt a flush of heat go through her limbs, and then, collecting herself, reminded herself that of *course* Marc Derenz had looked at her like that—*he* was in role-play just as much as she was! She bestowed an air kiss upon Celine, whose face had contorted in fury at Tara's appearance.

'I just *adore* house-hunting! We'll have *such* fun together! I can't wait!' she gushed, ignoring the other woman's obvious anger at her presence there. 'Why not describe what you're after by way of a villa over drinks?' she invited Celine cordially, hoping that Marc Derenz would lead them to wherever it was that cocktails were going to be served. She hadn't a clue—and if Celine realised that it might give the game away.

Thankfully, he did just that, ushering them both into a sumptuous Art Deco salon, where wide French windows opened onto a terrace bathed in late sunshine. Celine, all but snatching her glass, immediately started to talk animatedly in German to Marc, clearly intent on cutting out Tara as much as she could.

Marc's expression was still radiating the same

thunderous displeasure it had been since he had seen Celine arrive without her husband. For her part, Tara cast a jaundiced eye at the woman.

Honey, you'd be welcome to him! He's arrogant and bad-tempered and totally charmless! Help yourself, do!

But of course that was out of the question. So, knowing she had to act—quite literally—she stepped forward, a determined smile on her face, placing a quite clearly possessive, hand on Marc Derenz's arm.

'I'm hopeless at German!' she announced insouciantly. 'And my French is only schoolgirl, alas. Are you telling Marc what you're looking for in a house here?'

As she spoke she was aware that the arm beneath her fingertips had steeled, and his whole body had tensed at her moving so closely into his body space. She pressed her hand on his sleeve warningly. Celine was never going to be fooled if she stayed a mile distant from him.

And he needn't think she *wanted* to be in his body space! His utterly unnecessary warning from the afternoon echoed in her head, informing her that she was to remember she was only here to *act* a part. Not to believe it was real.

I wouldn't want it to be real anyway, sunshine, she said tartly but silently to him.

In her head—treacherously—a single word hovered. *Liar.*

You might not like him, the voice went on, *but for some damn reason he has the ability to turn your knees to jelly, so you just be careful, my girl!*

She pushed it out. It had no place in her thoughts. None at all. She was *not* looking for Marc Derenz to pay her what he so clearly imagined would be the immense compliment of desiring her for real. So there was no need at all for him to have warned her off.

And all this—all she was going to have to act out for the duration—was just that. An act. Nothing more.

An act it might be, but it was hard going for all that.

All through dinner she made a relentless effort to be Marc Derenz's charming hostess—attentive to his guest, endlessly gushing and smiling about the delights of searching for zillion-dollar homes on the French Riviera to this woman who clearly wished her at the bottom of the ocean.

Tara was doggedly undeterred by Celine's barely civil treatment. Far more exasperating to her was Marc Derenz's stony attitude.

OK, so maybe he was still blazingly furious that Celine had turned up on her own, but that didn't mean he could get away with monosyllabic responses and a total lack of interest in the conversation Tara was so determinedly keeping going.

As they finally returned to the salon for coffee and liqueurs, she hissed at him, 'I can't do this all on my own! For heaven's sake, play *your* part as well!'

She slipped her hand into his arm and sat herself down with him on an elegant sofa, deliberately placing a hand on his muscled thigh. She felt him flinch, as if she'd burnt him, and a spurt of renewed irritation went through her. If *she* could do this, damn it, so could he!

She turned to him, liqueur glass in her hand. 'Marc, darling, you're being such a grouch! *Do* lighten up!' she cooed cajolingly.

Her reward was a dark, forbidding flash of his eyes, and an obvious increase in the reading on his displeasure meter as his expression hardened. Her mood changed abruptly. Actually, she realised, there was something very satisfying in winding up Marc Derenz! He was so *easy* to annoy.

A little frisson went through her. She might be playing with fire, but it was enticing all the same…

She turned back to Celine, who was fussing over her coffee. 'Marc's just sulking because he doesn't want to go house-hunting,' she said lightly. 'Men hate that sort of thing—let's leave him behind and do it ourselves!'

But Celine was having none of this. 'You know nothing about the area,' she said dismissively. 'I need Marc's expertise. Of course ideally,' she went on, 'we'd love to buy here, on Cap Pierre—it's *so* exclusive.'

'So much so that there is nothing changing hands,' was Marc's dampening reply.

Dieu, the last thing he wanted was Celine Neuberger anywhere on the Cap. And the next last thing he wanted, he thought, his mood darkening even more, was Tara's hand on his thigh.

It was taking all his resolve to ignore it. To ignore her, as he had been trying to do ever since his eyes had gone to her, descending the staircase with show-stopping impact, and he'd caught his breath at her beauty, completely unable to drag his eyes away from her.

All his adjurations to himself that Tara Mackenzie was out of bounds to him had vanished in an instant, and he'd spent the rest of the evening striving to remember them. But with every invasion by her of his personal space it had proved impossible to do so. As for her hissing at him like that just now—did she not realise how hard it was for him to have to remember this was only a part he was playing? And then, dear God, she had placed a hand on his thigh…

How the hell am I going to get through this week? Was I insane to bring her here?

But it didn't matter whether he had been insane or not—he was stuck with this now. And, tormenting or not, she was right. He had to behave as if he were, indeed, in the throes of a torrid affair with her—or else what was the point of her being here at all?

So, now, trying to make the gesture casual, he placed his free hand over hers. Was it her turn to tense suddenly? Well, *tough*.

To take his mind off the feel of her slender fingers beneath the square palm of his hand, he said, making his voice a tad more amenable, 'I'm sure you and Hans will find what you're looking for, though, Celine. How about higher on the coastline, with a view?'

Pleased at being addressed directly, even if did cast a sour look at him all but holding hands with Tara, Celine smiled engagingly.

'A view would be essential!' she stipulated, and then she was away, waxing lyrical about various houses she had details for, animatedly wanting to discuss them.

Marc let her run on, saying what was necessary when he had to, aware that the focus of his consciousness was actually the fact that his fingers had—of their own accord, it seemed—wound their way into Tara's... His thumb was idly stroking the back of her hand, which felt very pleasant to him, and her palm seemed be hot on his leg, which felt more than merely pleasant...

He could feel himself starting to wish Celine to perdition—and not for the reason that he had no interest whatsoever in a spot of adultery with his friend's wife...

Because he wanted Tara to himself...

He could feel his pulse quicken, arousal beckon...

Maybe the cocktail he'd imbibed, the wine he'd drunk over dinner, the brandy now swirling slowly in his glass, had loosened his inhibitions, faded the reminder he'd been imposing on himself all evening that he had not brought Tara here for any purpose other than to shield him from Hans's wife.

But what if I had?

The thought played in his mind, tantalising... tempting.

Then, with a douche of cold water, he hauled his thoughts away. He lifted his hand away too, restoring Tara's hand to her own lap with a casual-seeming move. He got to his feet. He needed to get out of here.

'Celine, forgive me. I have a call booked to a client in the Far East.' He hadn't, but he had to call time on this.

Celine looked put out, but he couldn't care less. Tara was looking up at him questioningly. Then she took the cue he was signalling. He saw her give a little yawn.

'We'd probably both better call it day,' she announced to Celine. 'I'm sure you're tired after your journey.'

She was making it impossible for Celine to linger, and Marc ushered them both from the room, bidding his unwanted guest goodnight.

Then he turned to the woman who was not his guest, but his temporary employee, however hard she was making it to remember that.

'I'll be about half an hour, *mon ange*,' he murmured, knowing he had to give just the right impression to Celine. Knowing, with a part of his mind to which he was not going to pay any attention, that, however much of a siren call it was, he did not want it to be a mere 'impression' at all...

He silenced his mind ruthlessly, by force of will, turning on his heel and heading for his office, where he was *not* about to make phone call to the Far East, but another, far more urgently needed communication.

The whole evening had been nothing but a gruelling ordeal—and not just for the reasons he'd thought it would be. Not just because of Celine.

Because of Tara.

And what she was tempting him to.

Which he must resist or risk breaking the most essential rule he lived by.

As Tara gained her bedroom relief filled her. Dear Lord, but that had backfired on her—big-time! Hissing like that at Marc to be more convincing in his role-play! Had she been nuts to demand that? To take the initiative he would not?

Memory was hot in her head, as if it were still happening—sitting up close and personal beside him, so that the heat from his body was palpable through the fine jersey of her dress. And then, after so stupidly getting a kick out of winding him up with her taunt about being a grouch, putting her hand on his thigh.

Hard muscle and sinew…and a strength beneath the material of his trousers that had made her want to snatch her hand away as if she'd touched white-hot metal. But she hadn't been able to, because his own hand had closed over hers, imprisoning it between the hard heat of his thigh and the soft heat of his palm.

And then she'd felt her throat catch as that casual meshing of his fingers with hers, that slow, sensual stroking of his thumb, had lit up a thousand trembling nerve-ends in her…

No! Don't think about it! Focus, instead, on getting to bed.

Tomorrow was going to be another long day. Just putting up with Celine was ordeal enough—let alone Marc as well.

Putting him out of her mind as best she could,

she got on with getting into her night attire, carefully hanging up the beautiful dress she'd been wearing, then removing her make-up and brushing out her hair. The familiar rituals were soothing to her jagged nerves—as much as they *could* be soothed.

Aware that she was still on edge, and knowing why and deploring it, but unable to calm herself any more, she headed for the palatial en suite bathroom to brush her teeth. As she did so she glanced askance at the door inset beside it. It was no surprise that she'd been put into a bedroom with what must be a communicating door to wherever it was that Marc Derenz slept, because otherwise it would look too obvious that she wasn't really there in the role she claimed. But all the same it was unnerving to think that only a flimsy door separated her from him.

Without thinking too much about what she was doing, let alone why, she went to test it. Locked— and from the other side. A caustic smile pulled at her mouth. Oh, it was definitely time to remind herself that whatever Marc Derenz did in public in order to put out the impression that they were having an affair, in private he was obviously keeping to the arrogant warning he'd given her—not to take his attentions for real…

Well, that was a two-way message, and it was time to remind him of it! She reached for the bolt on her own side, meaning to shoot it closed. And jumped back.

The door had been pulled open from the other

side, and Marc Derenz was stepping through into her bedroom.

Her eyes flashed in alarm. 'What are you doing?' she demanded.

She saw his brows snap together in his customary displeased fashion, as if she had no business challenging his walking in unannounced to her bedroom. Quite illogically, she welcomed it.

It's better to dislike him than to—

Her disturbing thought was cut short.

'I need to speak to you,' he announced peremptorily.

He was still in his dinner trousers, but he'd taken off his jacket and his tie was loosened. It gave him a raffish look. As did the line of shadow clearly discernible along his jawline.

Tara felt her stomach hollow. It just did not matter how disagreeable he was. Marc Derenz really should not be so bone-meltingly attractive...

And he shouldn't be in your bedroom either.

The realisation hit her and she took a step back, suddenly aware that she was in her pyjamas. Oh, they might be modesty itself, with their wide silk trousers and high-collared *cheong-sang* top, but they were still nightwear.

'Well?' she prompted, lifting her chin. She didn't like the way his dark eyes had swept over her, then veiled instantly. Didn't like the way she was burningly aware that they had... Didn't like, most of all, the way her nerves had started to jangle all over again...

'I've been emailing Bernhardt—Hans's son.' Marc's voice was brusque, as if he wanted to get this over and done with. 'I've told him in no uncertain terms that he must make sure Hans joins us. I won't have Celine here on her own. Even with you here to—'

'To protect you,' completed Tara helpfully.

Another of his dark looks was his reply, before he continued as if she had not interrupted him. 'Thankfully Bernhardt agrees with me. He's going to tell his father he'll stand in for him at a board meeting so Hans can arrive tomorrow evening. It's all arranged.'

She could hear relief in his voice, and saw a snap of satisfaction in his eyes.

'So we just have to get through tomorrow, do we? Trailing along while Celine looks at houses?' Tara said.

She was trying to silence the jangling of her nerves at his unexpected presence—in her bedroom, with her only in her night attire. She fought to make her voice normal, as composed as she could make it.

'Or are you going to find a way of getting out of it? I don't mind coping with her on my own if you want to bottle it,' she added helpfully.

His expression darkened again. 'No, I'll have to come along as well. If I don't she'll end up landing Hans with some overpriced monstrosity!' He gave an exasperated sigh.

Tara couldn't help but give a laugh, though it earned her yet another darkling look. 'I'll take a bet she'll go for the most garish, opulent pile she can find,' she said, preferring to have a dig at Celine than let herself be distracted by Marc Derenz's overpowering, and utterly unfairly impactful presence in her bedroom. 'Gold bathrooms and crystal chandeliers in the kitchen.'

'Very likely,' he replied grimly. 'Oh, hell, why on earth did he marry the damn woman?' he muttered to himself.

'Well, she's certainly a looker,' Tara conceded, still trying to make normal conversation. 'Over-done-up, to my mind, but presumably it appeals to your friend.'

He shook his head. 'Not Hans,' he said. 'The last thing he wants is any kind of trophy wife.'

Tara couldn't keep the caustic note from her voice. 'Are you sure? Most men like to show off the fact that they can acquire a woman that other men will envy them for.'

Marc's eyes narrowed. 'Is that your experience?'

She shrugged her shoulders. 'It's pretty common in the world I come from—models are, after all, the ultimate trophy females to make a man look successful.'

Was there bitterness in her voice? She hoped not, but being with Jules had made her wary. What would a man like Marc know, or care, about men like Jules, who needed to feel big by draping a model on their arm? *He* certainly wouldn't need to.

A man as rich and as drop-dead gorgeous as he is doesn't need to prove a thing to anyone!

The thought was in her head before she realised it was there.

Then it was wiped right from her mind. Marc Derenz had taken a step towards her.

'Can you blame them?'

There was something different in his voice, in his stance, in the way he was looking at her.

Suddenly, out of nowhere, every nerve in her body was jangling again—louder than ever. What the hell was she doing, talking to him like this? Standing here in her bedroom, wearing only her silk pyjamas, while Marc Derenz stood there far too close to her, looking so unutterably damn *sexy* with his loosened tie, his jacketless shirt, the hint of a shadowed jawline...

She caught the scent of his aftershave—something expensive, custom-designed, a signature creation made for him alone...

And his eyes—those deep, dark eyes—like slate, but suddenly not hard like slate, but as if a vein of gold had suddenly been exposed in their unyielding surface...

She couldn't drag her own eyes from them...

Couldn't drag breath into her lungs...

Could not focus on a single other thing in the universe than those dark, gold-lit eyes resting on her...

The room seemed to be shrinking—or was it the space between them?

He started towards her again, lifted a hand. She caught the glint of gold at his cuffs, echoing that same glint in those dark eyes of his that were now holding hers...holding her immobile, breathless, so she couldn't breathe, couldn't move...

She could only hear the blood surging in her veins,

feel electricity crackle over her skin, as if all he had to do was touch her—make contact…

'Can you blame them?' he said again.

And now there was a husk in his voice, a timbre to it that did things to her insides even as his out-stretched hand reached towards her, a single finger drawing down her cheek, lingering at her mouth.

His eyes were playing over her face and she felt a kind of drowning weakness slacken her limbs. Making it quite impossible for her to move a muscle, to do anything other than simply stand there…stand there and feel the slow drift of his fingertip move across the soft swell of her lips. Only his touch on her mouth existed…only the soft, sensuous caress…

'Pourquoi es-tu si, si belle?' His murmur was a low husk as he lifted his other hand to slide it slowly, sensuously, around the nape of her neck, through the tumbled masses of her loosened hair. 'Why is it that I cannot resist your beauty?'

She felt her eyelids flutter, felt her pulse beating in her throat, felt her lips parting even as his fingers splayed across her cheek, cupped her jaw to tilt her face to his lowering mouth which she could not, for all the world, resist…

Her eyelids dropped across her eyes, veiling him from sight. She was reduced only to the kiss he was easing across the mouth she lifted to his… Reduced only to the feathered silk of his touch, the hand at her nape cradling her skull, the fingers woven into her hair.

It was like that lingering wrist-kiss all over again,

but a thousand times more so. A million sensations swirled within her at the sheer velvet sensuality of his kiss…his mouth moving on hers, tasting her, exploring her. She was helpless—helpless to resist. The heady scent of his aftershave, his body, was in her senses, in the closeness of him as he shaped her mouth to his.

She felt herself leaning into him, letting her own hands glide around the strong column of his back, feeling the play of muscle and sinew, with only the sheer cotton of his shirt to separate her palms from the warmth of his flesh.

She could not stop—would not. Blood was surging in her…her pulse was soaring. She was drowning in his kiss, unable to stop herself, unable to draw away, to find the sanity she needed to find…

And then, abruptly, he was pulling away from her. Stepping away so sharply that her hands fell from him, limp at her sides, just as her whole body felt limp.

Dazedly, Tara gazed blankly at him. She had no strength—none. All her limbs were slack and stricken. Inside her chest her heart was pounding, beating her down.

She heard him speak, but now there was no husk in his voice, no low, sensual timbre. Only a starkness that cut like a knife.

'That should not have happened.'

She felt it like a slap—but it was a sudden awakening from her deathly faint and her eyes flared back into vision, her mind into full consciousness of what she had permitted…given herself up to…

She saw him standing there, stepped back from him. There was a darkness in his face, in his eyes, and his features were pulled taut—as forbidding and shuttered as she had ever seen them.

Then, with the same sharp movement with which he'd pulled away from her, he was turning away, body rigid, his expression still tight as steel wire, walking with heavy, rapid strides to the door. Walking through. Snapping it shut behind him. Without another word.

Leaving her alone, heart pounding, lungs airless, his words echoing in her head—resonating as if it had been she who'd uttered them.

Dismay hollowed her.

Marc plunged down the staircase. *Dieu*, had he been insane to let that happen? Hadn't he warned himself repeatedly that he must keep his response to her hammered down, where it could not escape?

Anger with himself consumed him. Anger he welcomed—for it blotted out more than any other emotion could, blotted out the memory of that irresistible kiss.

Well, you should have resisted it! You should— and must—resist her! She is not here for such a purpose! It would be madness to indulge yourself. Indulge her...

Every reason for his warnings to himself about the dangerous folly of letting the desire that had seized him from the first moment her show-stopping beauty had hit upon his senses marched through his head at his command.

He kept them marching. He must allow nothing else to occupy his mind. Nothing except work. That would keep him on the straight and narrow.

Gaining the hallway, he yanked open the door to his office. The Far Eastern markets would soon be starting up. They would absorb him until he was sufficiently tired to risk heading for bed. *Tout seul.*

His mouth tightened. Most definitely alone.

And it must stay that way. Anything else was a folly he would not commit.

Would not.

CHAPTER FIVE

TARA STOOD IN the over-hot garden of the over-ornate villa they'd just toured, feigning an enthusiasm she did not feel in the slightest. But that was preferable to letting her thoughts go where she did not want them to go. To the memory of that disastrous kiss last night.

She gave a silent groan. Had she been crazy to let Marc Derenz kiss her? *Why* had she let him? Why hadn't she stopped him? Why hadn't she told him to go to hell? Why…?

Why did I kiss him back?

That was what was so disastrous—that she'd *let* him kiss her. And returned it!

Angrily, she catalogued all the reasons why she had been so insanely stupid as to have let that kiss happen. Capping it with the one she'd always had to remember, ever since she'd made the mistake of trusting Jules.

Men who see me only as a model are bad news! And I won't be any man's trophy to show off! I won't!

But even as she yanked that warning into her head she felt it wavering. Hadn't she already accepted that

Marc Derenz had no need of a trophy female—not with his wealth, his looks.

Yes, and doesn't that just make him even worse? she shot back to herself. *Thinking every woman in the world is after him?*

She pressed her lips together. Well, not her! She had *not* needed that final warning from him in the slightest.

'That should not have happened.'

And it wasn't going to happen again—that was for certain! Somehow, whatever it took, she was going to get through the rest of this week, collect her money and get away—away from the wretched man.

Until then she had to keep going.

She put her mind back to the role she was supposed to be playing.

'Four of the bedrooms don't have balconies,' she pointed out to Celine helpfully. 'Do you think that rules this one out?'

Celine ignored her. It had been obvious to Tara that she'd been doing her best to do so all morning. Instead she turned to Marc.

'What do *you* think, Marc, *cherie*?' she posed with a little pout. 'Does it matter if not all the bedrooms have balconies?'

'No,' said Marc succinctly, his indifference to the issue blatant. He glanced at his watch impatiently. 'Look, would you not agree that it's time for lunch?' he demanded. He was clearly at the limit of his patience.

Tara found herself almost smiling, and welcomed

the release from the self-punishing thoughts going round and round in her head. He was so visibly bored and irritated—and, whilst she could not blame him, she knew with a waspish satisfaction that this time it was not she who was drawing his ire. Besides, at least when he was being bad-tempered he wasn't being amorous...

His ill humour, she noted with another caustic smile, seemed completely lost on the armour-plated Celine however. All through lunch—at a very expensive restaurant in Nice—Tara watched the woman determinedly making up to him, constantly touching his sleeve with her long scarlet nails, making cooing noises at him, laughing in an intimate fashion and throwing fluttering little glances at him...

All to utterly no avail.

He sat there like a block of stone, his expression getting darker and darker, until Tara wanted to laugh out loud. She herself was doing her level best to drag Celine's attention towards her instead, chattering away brightly, waxing lyrical about the houses they'd viewed, the ones they might still view, obdurately not letting Celine blank her as the woman kept trying to do.

That her brightly banal chatter was only adding to the visible irritation on Marc's face did not bother her. What else did he expect her to do, after all? She was here to run interference, and that was what she was doing. And, after all, the way wretched Celine was behaving, the whole situation was just ridiculous! He really needed to lighten up about it.

As the woman turned away now, to complain about something or other to a hapless passing waiter, Tara could not suppress a roll of her eyes at Celine's endless plays for Marc's attention. Then, abruptly, his eyes snapped to hers, catching her in mid-eye-roll.

She saw his mouth tighten and one of his laser looks come her way. She gave a minute shake of her head in resignation, a sardonic twitch of her lips, and for a moment—just the slightest moment—she thought she saw something flicker in the slate-grey depths of his eyes. Something that went beyond a warning to her not to come out of role. Something that she had never seen before. A flicker so faint she could not believe she'd seen it.

Humour.

Good grief, did the wretched man actually have a sense of humour? Somewhere buried in the recesses of his rock-like personality?

If he did she didn't catch any more sight of it. After lunch was finally over Celine gushingly begged Marc to head for Monte Carlo. With ill grace he complied, and Tara found herself glad of the excursion. Not only was it a lot better than looking at over-priced, over-decorated villas for sale, but she'd never seen Monte Carlo, and she looked around her with touristic scrutiny at the grandeur of the Place de Casino, her gaze lingering on the fabled casino itself.

'It's where fools go to lose their money,' a sardonic voice said at her side.

She glanced at Marc, whose expression mirrored his disparaging tone of voice. 'Now, *there* speaks the sober banker!' she exclaimed lightly. 'All the same,' she added, 'sometimes those fools come out millionaires.'

'The winners win from the other gamblers who lose.' His tone was even more crushing. 'There is no free money in this world.'

'Unless,' Tara could not resist saying, 'one marries it… That's always been a favourite way of getting free money.'

Her barb was wasted. Celine's attention was focussed only on the luxury shopping mall opposite the casino. Like a heat-seeking missile, she headed towards it. As Tara made to follow she caught a frown on Marc's face. She presumed it was because he was now facing a prospect every man loathed—shopping with women.

Impulsively, she tucked her hand into his elbow. *'Courage, mon brave!'* she murmured humorously, leaning into him.

She only meant to lighten him up, maybe even to catch a glimpse of that crack in his steel armour that she'd evoked so unexpectedly over lunch. But clearly his mood had worsened too much for that.

Her hand was abruptly removed and he strode forward, leaving her to hasten after him into the mall.

She gave a sigh. And a twist of her mouth. It had been stupid of her to do that. And not because it had annoyed him instead of lightening him up. Because *any* physical contact at all with the man was not a good idea in the least…

Not after last night. Not after that kiss—that disastrous, dangerous, completely *deranged* kiss that she should never have let happen!

No, any physical contact with him that wasn't forced on her by the necessity of playing the role he was paying her to play, was totally *défendu*. Totally forbidden. And she mustn't forget it. Not even to wind the man up. Or try and lighten him up. It was just too risky...

Because, however overbearing and obnoxious he could be, she was just too damned vulnerable to what he could make her feel.

Sobered, she followed him into the mall.

'*Fraulein*, how very good to meet you!'

Hans Neuberger was shaking Tara's hand genially, his face smiling. He had a nice face, Tara decided. Not in the least good-looking, and late middle-aged—a good twenty years older than his wife—but with kindly eyes.

She smiled warmly back. 'Herr Neuberger,' she returned.

'Hans, please!' he said immediately, and she liked him the more.

They were in the magnificent Art Deco salon once more, and Hans Neuberger had just arrived. He'd kissed Celine dutifully on the cheek, but she'd turned away impatiently. Tara thought her a fool to treat her kindly husband with such open indifference.

'Hans! I'm glad to see you!'

Tara turned. Marc was striding in, holding out his

hand to his guest in greeting. She stared, disbelief etching her features.

Good God, the man could smile! As in *really* smile! Not the cynical, humourless indentation of his mouth she'd seen so far, or that infinitesimal chink she'd seen at lunchtime, but an actual smile! A smile that parted his mouth, reached his eyes to crinkle them at the edge. That lightened his entire face...

She felt her breath catch.

Gone, totally, was the hard-faced, bored, impatient, ill-tempered expression she was so used to. Just... gone. It made him a *completely* different person—

She reeled with it, still hardly believing what she was seeing. And she felt something shift inside her, rearrange itself. Marc Derenz...*smiling!* It was like the sun coming out after thunderclouds...

She stared on, bemused, aware that her pulse had suddenly quickened and that it had something to do with the way Marc's smile had softened his face, warmed his eyes... It warmed something in her as well, even though it was not directed at her in the least.

But what if it were—?

No. She shut her mind off. It was bad enough coping with the utterly unfair impact the man had on her when he was being his usual ill-humoured self. She could not possibly think how she would cope if he were capable of being *nice*, for heaven's sake!

It was a resolve she had to stick to throughout dinner. She was helped in that by focussing her attention on Celine's husband. Hans Neuberger really was far too nice to be landed with a shrew like Celine. He was clearly hurt and bewildered by her dismissiveness, and Tara did her best to divert him.

'I think Marc said you're based in Frankfurt? All I know about it is the huge annual book fair. Oh, and that it was the birthplace of Goethe.'

Hans's kindly face lit up. 'Indeed—our most famous son! And Germany's most famous poet—'

Celine's voice was sharp as she cut across him. 'Oh, for heaven's sake, Hans, don't start boring on about poetry! Who cares?'

The rudeness was so abrupt that Tara stared. Hans was silenced, looking stricken. Tara felt immensely sorry for him and rallied to his defence.

'I'm afraid I know very little about German poetry—it didn't really come into my English Literature course at university, alas,' she said politely.

'Speaking of university…' Marc's voice interjected now, as he picked up the baton. 'Has your youngest—Trudie—graduated yet?'

As Hans answered Tara saw Marc throw a glance at her. There was something in his eyes she'd never seen before. Appreciation. Appreciation, evidently, for coming to Hans's rescue as she had.

She blinked for a moment. Then gave a minute nod.

For the rest of the meal she did her best to shield Hans from his unpleasant wife, drawing him out about Goethe and the German Romantics, comparing them with the English Romantics of the same period. Marc joined in, widening the discussion to include French poetry too, keeping the conversation going.

Celine seemed to be in a foul mood—though whether that was because she was clearly being cut out of a conversation she was incapable of contributing to, or whether it was just because her husband had arrived, Tara wasn't sure and didn't care.

What *was* clear, though, was that Celine was not about to let her husband's presence get in the way of her determined pursuit of Marc Derenz, and she was still focusing her attention solely on him.

She continued to do so, quite blatantly, the following day. She dragged them all out for yet more house-viewings, then insisted on heading to Cannes, so she could trawl through the luxury brand-name boutiques strung out along the Croisette.

'She really is,' Tara heard herself say *sotto voce* to Marc, as Celine preened in front of a mirror, 'the most tiresome woman ever! Poor Hans can't possibly want to stay married to her!'

'She's like a leech,' he snapped shortly. 'And Hans is too damn soft-hearted for his own good!'

'Can he really not see her true character?' Tara mused disbelievingly.

Marc's face hardened. 'Men can be fools over women,' he said.

She glanced at him curiously. He couldn't possibly be referring to himself—she knew that. A man like Marc Derenz was made of granite. No woman could make an impact on him.

'Marc, *cherie*!' Celine's piercing call sought to summon his attention. 'Your taste is impeccable! Should I buy this?'

'That is for Hans to say, not me,' came his tight reply.

'Oh, Hans knows nothing about fashion at all!' was Celine's rudely dismissive retort.

Tara stepped forward, seizing a handbag from a stand. 'This would go perfectly with that outfit,' she said. And it was not for Celine's sake, but for the sake of her hapless spouse, hovering by her side.

Celine was hesitating between outright rejection of anything that Tara suggested and lust for the shiny gold bag. The latter triumphed, and she snatched it from her.

'Magpie, as well as leech,' Tara murmured, her head dipped towards Marc.

Did she hear a crack that might just be laughter break from him, before it was abruptly cut off? She stole a look at him, but the moment was gone.

At least, though, the handbag had clinched it and Celine was ready to depart.

It still took for ever, it seemed to Tara—and probably to Marc and Hans as well, she thought cynically—before they could finally return to the villa. Another grim evening loomed ahead of them, with Celine openly discontented because Marc had flatly vetoed her repeated suggestion that they head for the casino at Monte Carlo.

But her petulant mood improved markedly when, after dinner, she took a phone call that made her announce, 'That was the Astaris. They're on their yacht in Cannes. They're giving a party tomorrow.' A frown crossed her brow. 'I haven't got a *thing* to wear for it!' She turned towards Marc. '*Do* run me into Monte, tomorrow, *cherie*! I'm sure Tara can stay here and discuss poetry with Hans,' she added pettishly.

Not surprisingly, Celine's blatant ploy to get Marc to herself for yet another shopping expedition failed, and the following morning all four of them set out for Monaco.

This time, thankfully, Celine availed herself of a personal shopper, who read her client perfectly so that she could emerge triumphantly with a gown that would cost her husband an outrageous sum of money. Full of herself, Celine then demanded that they lunch at the principality's premier hotel, overlooking the marina packed with luxury yachts, and proceeded to plague her husband to buy something similar.

It was obvious to Tara that this was the last thing Hans wanted to do, and she took pity on him by deliberately interrupting the flow of his wife's importuning.

'Tell me,' she asked, 'what else is in Monte Carlo besides the casino, luxury shops and yachts?'

Hans's face brightened. 'The Botanic Gardens are world-famous,' he said.

'Have we time to visit?' Tara asked. It would be nice, after all, she thought, sighing inwardly, while she was here, actually to see something of the Côte d'Azur other than expensive villas, expensive shops and expensive restaurants.

'What a good idea!' Celine put in immediately. 'Hans, you take Tara to the gardens and Marc and I can—'

'I thought you wanted to talk to a yacht broker?'

Marc cut across her brutally, pre-empting whatever scheme Celine was about to dream up to get him on his own.

Celine sulked visibly, then ordered Hans off to find out who the best yacht broker in the principality was. Dutifully the poor man went off to ask the hotel's concierge. Perking up at her husband's absence—however temporary—Celine leant across to Marc, resting her hand on his sleeve in her possessive fashion, stroking it seductively.

'A yacht is *so* essential these days—you must agree!' she oozed. '*Do* help me persuade Hans, *cherie!*'

There was a cajoling, caressing note in her voice, and her scarlet nails curved over his arm. Her over-made-up face was far too close to his, her eyes greedy for him, openly lascivious—and suddenly, out of nowhere, Tara had had enough. Just *enough*.

There was something in her that absolutely revolted at seeing Celine paw at Marc the way she did. Something that was the last thing she should feel about him—but feel it she did, and with a power that shook her.

Parting her lips in an acid grimace she leant forward. 'Celine,' she said, sweetly, but with a bite to her voice that could have cut through steel wire, 'call me old-fashioned, but I would prefer you, please, to take your hand *off* Marc!'

Immediately Celine's eyes snapped to Tara. There was venom in them. And in the words she snapped out too.

'Oh, my, how *very* possessive! Anyone might think you have *ideas* about him!'

It was a taunt—an obvious one—and Tara opened her mouth to retaliate. Except no words came. Only a spearing dart of emotion that should not be there... should not exist at all.

And then, suddenly, Marc's voice cut across her consciousness. She felt her hand being taken, turned over, exposing her wrist. Before she knew what he intended he had dipped his head, grazed his mouth across that tender skin, sending a million nerve-endings firing in her so that she could only stare at him, eyes widening...

'I very much hope Tara *does* have ideas about me... very possessive ideas!' she heard him say. 'For I most certainly do about her!'

His voice had dropped to a low purr, and now his gaze was holding Tara's with an expression of abso-lute intentness.

Was he trying to convey a message? She didn't know—could only feel all those nerve-endings still firing inside her like a hail of fireworks as the dark gaze on her suddenly lifted, shifting to Celine. Tara felt his hand, large and strong, enfold hers, meshing his fingers into hers...*possessively.*

She saw him smile—a smile, she suddenly thought, that had a twist of ruthlessness to it. A ruth-lessness that was entirely explained when she heard him speak.

'You can be the first to know, Celine.' That same deep, steely purr was in his voice. 'Tara is my fiancée,'

Fiancée? Tara heard the word, but could not credit it. Where had *that* come from?

Urgently, she looked at Marc, burningly conscious not just of what he had dropped like a concrete block on them all, but even more of the tightly meshed fingers enclosing hers. Possessively…very possessively.

With a corner of her consciousness she heard a hissing intake of breath from Celine.

'*Fiancée?* Don't be absurd!'

Her derision stung. Stung with an echo of Marc's voice telling her not to get ideas about him, telling her this was playacting only and for no other purpose.

And it stung with much more. With the way his mouth had felt like velvet on the tender skin of her wrist just now, taunting her…tempting her…

Of its own volition and entirely instinctively, with an instinct as old as time and as powerful as the desire she felt for the man who had brought her here, Tara felt her mouth curve into a derisive smile, a mocking laugh.

Because he did not desire her for himself, but only to block another woman's access to him.

She felt her hand lift to Marc's cheek, felt herself lean towards him. Felt her mouth reach for his, open to his, to feast on it, possessive with passion and naked desire…

How long she kissed him she did not know, for time had stopped, had ceased to exist. There was only the sensation of Marc's mouth, exploding within her, the taste of him, the scent of him, the weakening of every part of her body as desire flamed inside her…

Dazed, she drew back, gathering what senses she could, knowing her heart was pounding in her breast but that she had to say something. Anything.

Deliberately she gave that mocking little laugh again. Clearly Celine had wanted proof of the engagement Marc had suddenly and out of nowhere imposed upon the scene.

'We were going to keep it secret—weren't we, darling?'

Her glance at Marc was brief. She did not meet his eyes...did not dare to. Then she looked back to Celine across the table. She had to stay in role, in character—that was essential, however hectic her pulse was after that insanely reckless kiss that she had been unable to prevent herself from taking from him.

'Don't say anything to Hans, will you?' she said to Celine. 'Marc wants to tell him himself—before we announce it formally.'

The expression on Celine's face was as if she had swallowed a scorpion—or a whole bucketful of them. Then Hans was coming back to the table. He started to say something about yacht brokers but Celine cut across him. She was furious—absolutely seething.

Tara's glance went treacherously to the man she had just kissed with such openly passionate abandon...

But then so was Marc...

CHAPTER SIX

MARC YANKED ON his DJ and strode to the connecting door, pulling it open and striding into Tara's bedroom. He still could not believe he'd done what he'd done. Telling Celine that Tara was his fiancée! And then letting her kiss him—*again*. Had he gone mad? He must have. But had there been *any* other way of getting Hans's damn wife to lay off him?

Even as he'd made that momentous announcement he'd been appalled at himself. Danger had shimmered all around. Every precept he'd lived his life by had been appalled.

And now he had to do what he was intent on doing—make it absolutely crystal-clear to Tara Mackenzie that he had spoken entirely on impulse, exasperated beyond the last of his patience by Celine. It was a final means to an end—nothing more than that. Being his fiancée was every bit as fictional as his original proposition.

His mouth set in a grim expression. That devastating kiss she'd given him had not been fictional in the least! It had been searingly, devastatingly *real*…

But he absolutely could *not* risk that. Risk anything like that at all! Not with Tara—the woman he should have nothing to do with whatsoever outside the playacting he was paying her for…

She can't be anything in my life—I can't risk it. And I can't risk her thinking she can be anything in my life. Wanting any of this to be real…

His eyes went to her now. She was sitting at the dressing table, putting on her lipstick. She was quite at home in his villa, in this bedroom with its luxurious atmosphere, with its priceless pieces of Art Deco furniture, the silver dressing table set, the walls adorned with paintings from the thirties by artists whose prices in auction rooms were stratospheric.

Tara looked perfect in the setting—as if she belonged there…

But she doesn't belong. I hired her to play a part, and the fact that the part has suddenly become that of my fiancée changes nothing!

That was what he had to remember.

That the searing desire he felt for her was not something he could permit.

Part of him registered that, yet again, she was looking totally stunning. The russet silk halter-necked evening gown left her sculpted shoulders bare and skimmed the slender contours of her spectacular body, and her glorious hair waved lustrously over her shoulders in rich abandon.

Her head swivelled sharply as he strode in, and she dropped her lipstick on a silver tray.

'We need to talk!' Marc's voice was brusquer than he'd intended, but he did not care.

Tara's chin lifted, her eyes defiant. She got to her feet and got in first. 'Don't look at me like that!' she said. 'I know I was impulsive, kissing you like that, but—'

He strode up to her, took her shoulders. He'd had to wait *hours* for this moment! He'd had to endure babysitting Hans at the yacht broker's so he didn't end up buying a damn yacht for his appalling wife, then endure the car ride back to the villa, and then endure Tara disappearing up to her room to shower and dress for the evening. He was not going to wait a single interminable moment longer!

'It was *totally* unnecessary!' he barked.

'It was totally *necessary*!' Tara shot back. She wrenched herself free. 'Look, you'd just dropped that on me out of the blue! Saying I was your fiancée! I didn't know what to do—only that I had to follow your lead and make it look real!'

'*Dieu*, it looked real, all right! It damn near earned a round of applause from everyone there! And, worse, it nearly got seen by Hans.' He took a rasping breath. 'Hans must *not* know anything about this—do you understand? Because it isn't real! You *do* understand that, don't you?'

His eyes were skewering hers and his hand slashed the air for emphasis.

'There is *no* relationship between us! *No* engagement! Do *not* think otherwise!'

He saw her expression tighten, her eyes flash.

'Of course I do!' she snapped.

'Then *behave* like you understand it!' he shot back. He drew a deep, if ragged, breath to calm himself, get himself back under iron control. Because if he didn't…

She was standing there, breasts heaving, eyes fired with retaliation, looking so incredibly beautiful that with a single impulse he could have swept her up into his arms and buried his mouth in hers, feasting on those lush, silken lips…

And he dared not—dared not do anything of the sort. It would be madness. All he could do was what he did now. School his features, take another breath…

He held up a hand, silencing any utterance she might be going to say. He needed to say his piece first. 'OK, so I dropped a bombshell…went off-script. And OK…' his expression changed '…if I must I can accept that you acted on impulse to give credibility to what I'd just thrown at you.'

His breathing was still heavy, but he forced it back. Went on with what he had to say.

'But from now on, although we've told Celine we're engaged, we absolutely *must not* let Hans think so!' He took another ragged breath, ran his hand through his hair. 'Or he will believe it.'

His mind slewed away from the prospect of Hans believing that he and Tara were engaged to be married… the hassle and misunderstanding it would lead to…the absolute impossibility of it ever being real, Hans would not understand.

That was what he must cling to now—the fact that

his outburst of sheer exasperated temper, when he had been goaded beyond endurance by Celine, was for *her* consumption only, serving only to convince her to give up any hopes of an adulterous affair with him.

'So,' he said now, 'are we clear on that? We've let Celine think we are engaged—that I've proposed to you and you've accepted—but, as you so adeptly persuaded her, that I am waiting to tell my old friend Hans myself, and we'll be announcing it formally later on. And on that basis…' he took a final heavy breath, his eyes skewering Tara '…we'll get on with the rest of this damn evening. Which I am *not* looking forward to—Celine's appalling friends and their even more appalling party to endure!'

He held out a hand to Tara, not wanting her to say a word…not wanting her to do anything but meekly go along with what he was paying her to do—acting the part of his fiancée.

For a moment it looked as if she was going to argue with him—something no employee of his had ever dared to do. And Tara was no different from *any* other employee—that was what he had to remember. What *she* had to remember.

Then stiffly, ignoring his outstretched hand, she marched to the door, pulled it open.

He caught up with her, and they walked down the stairs. *'Smile,'* Marc urged grimly, *sotto voce*, 'you're my secret fiancée, remember!'

He saw her mouth set in a smile—tight, but there, even if it *was* totally at odds with the glacial expression in her eyes.

As they walked into the salon he saw Celine was already there, looking gaudy in a new gold lamé gown, Hans, totally ignored by her, stood dutifully at her side.

A basilisk glare shot from Celine to Tara beside him, far stronger than any animosity she'd displayed so far towards the woman she perceived as getting in her way. Marc's mouth compressed tightly. Well, maybe his announcement and Tara's outrageous kiss had hit home—even if he was still furious that she'd had the temerity to do such a thing off her own bat.

His simmering anger—and the prospect of a party with a bunch of Celine's friends—made him stiffer than ever in his manner, and his 'Shall we set off?' was made through gritted teeth. His jaw tightened even more when he felt Tara slip her hand into his arm. And nor did his black mood improve when they boarded a yacht lit up like a Christmas tree, music blaring and the deck heaving with just the kind of people he disliked most—those who showed off their money as conspicuously and tastelessly as possible.

Celine, however, was clearly in her element, and she swanned around, discarding Hans as soon as she could, knocking back champagne as if it was water. Marc watched her flirting openly with other men and did his best to keep talking to Hans and to avoid as much as possible any contact with anyone else.

Including Tara.

He was burningly conscious of her standing at his side, not saying a great deal—partly because of the noise of the party and partly because he was quite deliberately talking business with Hans, attempting to block his friend's view of his wife, currently cavorting on the small dance floor with unconcerned abandon with some man. He had no idea who and doubted Hans did either.

But, for all his efforts to ignore Tara, he could still catch her elusive fragrance, hear the rustle of her gown as she shifted position, and he knew that he wanted only to turn his head so his eyes could feast on her...

Was it the hypnotic rhythm of the music, or the champagne he'd imbibed to get him through this ordeal, or the oh-so-occasional brush of her bare arm against his that was building up inside him a pressure he was finding it harder and harder to resist?

He didn't know—only knew that Tara standing beside him was a torment.

I want her. I should not want her, but I do. It's madness to want her, and I know it—and it makes no difference. Whatever it is about her, she makes me forget all the rules I've lived my life by...

'Marc, *cherie*, dance with me!'

Celine had abandoned her partner, was sashaying up to him. Her eyes were glittering and the overpowering scent of her perfume was cloying. She leaned towards him, as if to lead him out onto the dance floor.

'Dance with Hans,' he answered shortly. 'I'm about to dance with Tara.'

The moment he said it he regretted it. The last thing he needed to endure was taking Tara out on the dance floor. But it was too late. Celine's eyes flashed angrily at his blunt refusal as he turned to Tara.

'*Mon ange?* Shall we?' His voice was tight, and the expression in his eyes warned her not to refuse him.

He saw her stiffen, saw her obvious reluctance to be taken into his arms and danced with. It fuelled his anger. He reached out, helping himself to her bare arm, and guided her forward. Stiffly, she looped her arms around his neck, barely touching him, and his hands moved to rest on her slender hips.

He could feel the heat of her body through the thin fabric of her gown. Feel, too, how stiffly she was moving as they started to dance. He made himself look down at her face, which was set in stark lines, as if dancing with him were the most repugnant thing in the world.

'Celine is watching us,' he gritted. 'Let's make this a bit more believable, shall we? After all,' he added, 'we're an engaged couple now, aren't we? So give it all you've got, *mon ange.*'

His taunt was deliberate, and she knew it—he could see by the sudden flash in her eyes. It gave him a perverse satisfaction to see it, to know with every male instinct in him that there was only one reason why she was reluctant to make this look real.

And it was not because he repelled her...

It was time to make that clear to her—and if it helped convince Celine too...well, right now he didn't give a damn about Hans's benighted wife or keeping her away from him. Right now only one intention fuelled him. Consumed him...

His hands at her hips drew her towards him, closing the distance between them, and one palm slid to the small of her back to splay across her spine. The supple heat of her body was warm beneath his palm.

For a split second, he felt her resist—as if she would not give in to what he knew from the tremor that ran through her and the sudden flaring of her eyes her body was urging her to do. Then, with a little helpless sigh in her throat, her resistance was gone and she was folding against him, her hands tightening around his neck, her eyes gazing up at him.

He felt her breasts crest against his chest—felt his own body reacting as any male body would react to such a woman in his arms! A woman who was driving him crazy with wanting her, being denied her...

His splayed hand at her spine pinioned her to him and his thighs guided her in the slow, sensual rhythm of the dance. He heard her breath catch again. Her lips were close to his, so tantalisingly close. He felt his head dip...wanting so badly to feel that silken velvet he had tasted only once before. He hungered for it with a desire that was now surging in him, to taste her again...to sate himself on her...

He pulled her more closely against him, knowing that she knew—for how could she not know just how very much he desired her...?

His lashes dipped over his eyes. He said her name—low and husky with desire... Relief was flooding through him—relief that finally she was in his arms, in his embrace, that she was pressed as closely to him as her body would be were he making love to her…

The rest of the world had disappeared. Hans, Celine, the whole damn yacht had disappeared. Only Tara was here—the woman who had stopped the breath in his lungs the first time he'd set eyes on her. The woman he wanted now more than any other woman.

His eyes were holding hers, not relinquishing them, watching her pupils expanding, seeing the dilation of desire in those incredible blue-green eyes of hers…

His mouth lowered to hers, seeking the sweet, silk velvet of her lips…so hungry to feel them part for him…for her to yield the sweetness of her mouth to his once more… Desire was like molten lava in him…

And then, abruptly, she was yanking herself away from him, and there was something flaring in her eyes now that was not desire—that was the very opposite of that. She strained against him, dropping her arms from him, removing his hands from her body. She seemed to be swaying as he looked down at her, face dark with her rejection.

'The music has stopped.'

She got the words out as if each one were a stone. He stared at her blankly, then heard her go on, her eyes like knives now.

'And if you *ever* try that on again with me I'll… I'll…'

But she did not finish. Instead, with a sudden contortion of her face, she walked off the dance floor, seizing up a glass of champagne from a passing waiter and knocking it back.

'A lovers' tiff? Oh, dear!' Celine's voice was beside him, her false sympathy not concealing her spite.

He ignored her, his eyes only for Tara, clutching her flute, refusing to look at him. His senses were still aflame, afire, and yet as the noise of the party filled the air, as the thud of music started up again, faster this time, he turned to Hans.

'Let's get out of here,' he said bluntly.

Ruthlessly, he shepherded them ashore, summoning his driver as he did so, and then piling them all into the limo the moment it drew up.

Tara had got in first, and was making herself extremely busy with a seatbelt. Her colour was high, her mouth set tight, long legs slanted away from his direction. As he threw himself into his own seat—diagonally opposite Tara—he saw Celine's gaze whip between the two of them. Speculation was in them as she took in Tara's withdrawal, her hostile body language.

Marc shut his eyes. He was beyond caring now. Let Celine think whatever the hell she wanted! His thoughts were elsewhere.

He wouldn't get any sleep that night—it would be impossible—but he didn't care about that either...

The moment they arrived back at the villa Tara all but bolted up the stairs, and he heard her bedroom door slam shut. Hans also took himself off. Marc made for the sanctuary of his office—anything to get away from Celine, who had gone to help herself from the drinks trolley in the salon.

He was just pushing open his office door when he heard her call out behind him.

'Marc, *cherie*—my poor, poor sweet!'

He hauled himself around. Celine was issuing towards him, a liqueur glass in her hand. Her eyes were glittering as she made for him. Every muscle in his body tensed. His black mood instantly tripled in intensity. Dear God, this was the last thing he needed now.

'Celine, I have work to do,' he ground out.

She ignored him. Came to him. Draped one bare arm around his shoulder. Her over-sweet scent was nauseating to him, her powdered half-exposed breasts in the skin-tight gold dress even more so.

He yanked her arm away, propelled her backwards. She was undeterred. He could smell alcohol mingling with her perfume.

The glitter in her eyes intensified. 'Don't marry that woman, Marc. You can't! She's not right for you. You know she isn't. She thinks she can treat you the way she did tonight. Push you away. You don't want a woman like that, Marc!'

She swayed towards him, trying to reach for him again. He seized her wrist, holding her at a distance. His face was thunderous, but she was still trying to touch him, to clutch at him with her scarlet nails.

'You want *me*, Marc! I know you do!' she cried, her voice slurring, 'I would be so, *so* good for you! Let me show you.' She swayed again, as if to throw herself into his arms.

'Celine, you are married to Hans,' he growled.

Dear God in heaven, was he to endure this now? On top of everything else? Fighting off Celine, with her rampant libido loosened by the alcohol she'd consumed all evening?

Her face twisted. 'Hans?' She all but spat out the name. 'He means nothing to me! *Nothing!* I should never have married him! I can't bear him. I can't bear him to touch me! He's old and pathetic and boring!' Her voice was vicious, cruel. 'I want to divorce him! Get him out of my life! I want a man like *you*, Marc—only you!'

Marc thrust her from him, stepping aside, filled with disgust at her. 'Get to bed, Celine. Sleep it off. You are the last woman on this earth I'd be interested in, and I wouldn't be even if you weren't married to Hans!'

He heard her gasp in stunned disbelief and outrage, but he was turning away from her, plunging inside his office. Slamming the door shut behind him. He leant back against it, slipping the lock. Not trusting Hans's unspeakable wife not to try and follow him in.

He swore fluently. Cursing her. Cursing the whole world. Cursing, most of all, the fact that upstairs, in a bedroom he must not let himself go anywhere near, was the one woman on earth that he wanted.

Who was tormenting him beyond endurance.

Tara woke. Instantly awake after dreams she dared not remember.

I can't bear this! I can't bear this any longer!

To have to act this role with Marc—only act it! Act it and keep him at bay at the same time. To tell herself over and over again that it was just role-play, nothing more than that!

Except it wasn't, was it? She could no more fool herself that she was acting than she could tell herself that *he* was!

Memory burned in her of that slow dance to end all slow dances... Their own bodies had betrayed them, shown them that neither of them were *acting*...

No! She mustn't think of it! Must not remember it!

She was here for one reason only: to protect Marc Derenz from another man's wife. And she was doing it for money, as a paid employee. *Anything* else was not real.

Whatever their bodies told them.

She hauled her mind away. So what? So what if she could not stop her body's reaction to him? If she could not stop that electricity surging within her whenever he looked at her, touched her? It didn't matter—not a jot—because none of this was real.

And even if it were real, she told herself, her thoughts bleak now, she could not let it be real. She was an outsider to this world. Her life was in England and she was moving to the country, starting afresh, getting out of the fashion world. Out of the orbit of men like Marc Derenz.

However powerful and devastating his impact on her...

With a heavy sigh she got up, went through into

the en suite bathroom. There was another gruelling day ahead of her. She had better brace herself for it.

Yet as she headed downstairs a little while later she noticed there seemed to be a different atmosphere in the villa. It was quieter, for a start, and as she crossed the salon to reach the terrace where breakfast was always served she realised she could not hear Celine's dominating voice yapping away.

She walked out. There was only Marc, sitting in his usual place at the head of the table, drinking his coffee, perusing the morning newspapers.

Tara frowned. 'Where are Hans and Celine?' she asked as she took her seat. Her expected sense of awkwardness after the night before had vanished in her surprise at not seeing his guests there.

Marc looked up. He hadn't heard her step out on the terrace. His eyes went to her, riveting her like a magnet, then instantly veiling.

'They've gone,' he said.

Tara's frown deepened as she reached for the jug of orange juice. 'What do you mean? More house-viewing?'

Marc sat back, folded his newspaper and set it aside with a deliberate movement. His mood could not be more different from his mood when he had ploughed up the stairs last night, thrusting the vision of the drunken, vicious-mouthed harpy that was Celine from him, wanting only to seek oblivion from what Tara had so tormentingly aroused in him.

The news that had greeted him this morning had wiped all that from his mind, leaving only one emotion. And that had brought with it only one decision that now burned in him, just as the memory of Tara kissing him had, of how their bodies had clung to each other in that devastating slow dance...

With Celine and Hans gone, and Tara tormenting him with his desire for her, there was only *one* decision he now wanted to make—and to hell with all his endless damn warnings to himself! To hell with the lot of them!

She was gazing at him now... Tara with her sea-blue eyes set in that breathtakingly beautiful face of hers, her lush lips parted, a frown still on her brow as he answered her question.

'No,' he said.

The emotion he felt was in his voice, and he could see that it had registered with Tara as well, for her expression had changed.

'Gone,' he elaborated now. 'As in Hans has flown back to Frankfurt, where he will be consulting a divorce lawyer. As for Celine—I don't know and don't care. Presumably to find herself a divorce lawyer as well.'

Tara stared. *'Divorce?'*

'Yes.' Marc smiled.

And Tara, to her disbelief, realised that it was a genuine, hundred-carat smile.

It wasn't just the shock of what he'd said but the dazzling impact of his smile that froze the jug in her hand. 'I don't understand,' she said weakly.

He lifted his coffee cup again, tilted it towards her. 'Congratulations,' he said. 'To both of us! It did the trick—*my* announcement to Celine yesterday that you were my fiancée and *your* oh-so-convincing behaviour that went with it!'

He took a mouthful of coffee and continued in that voice that was so different from any she had heard from him before.

'It rattled Celine into making one last desperate attempt on me. When we got back last night she threw caution to the winds—and herself at me. Full-on. She told me she didn't want Hans any more, that she only wanted me. What I didn't realise at the time,' he went on, 'when I was disabusing her of her hopes, was that Hans overheard her saying she wanted to divorce him.' He took a breath. 'So he is going to oblige her and file for divorce himself.'

Tara's face lit. 'That's *wonderful*! I couldn't be happier for him!'

'Nor me,' said Marc. His expression changed again. 'Celine will try and take him to the cleaners, but Bernhardt will make sure she gets as little as possible. He's been on the phone to me already, thanking me profusely.'

His eyes rested on Tara. They were warm in a way she'd never seen before. So was his voice when he spoke again.

'And I have to thank you too, Tara.'

His expression was veiled suddenly and his voice suddenly changed again. Now there was something in it that sent flickers of electricity through her, that quickened her pulse, made her eyes fix on his.

'You don't need me to tell you how damnably tormenting this whole thing has been! But…' he gave a heartfelt sigh, rich with the profound relief that was the only emotion in him right now '…thank the Lord that is all over now!'

Inside his head Marc heard the very last of his lifelong warnings to himself—heard it and dismissed it. He had not come this far, endured this much, to listen to it any more. Hans and Celine were gone—but Tara… Oh, Tara was here—and here was exactly where he wanted her…

And whatever else he wanted of her—well, he was damn well going to yield to it. Resisting it any longer, resisting *her*, was just beyond him now. Totally beyond him. Yes, she was a woman he would never usually have allowed himself to get this close to physically, but fate had brought them this far and he was not going to deny any longer what was between them.

Up till now it had been playacting—but from this morning onwards, he would make it searingly, blazingly *real*. It was all he wanted—all that consumed him.

She was gazing at him now, with uncertainty in her face—and something more than that. Something that told him he was not going to be the only one giving in to what had flamed between them right from the very start.

He smiled a smile warm with anticipation. With the relief he felt not just at Celine's departure but at the thought of his own yielding to what he so wanted.

He poured himself some more coffee, helped himself to a brioche. 'Now,' he went on, 'we just have to decide how we're going to celebrate the routing of the unspeakable Celine.'

Tara looked at him. Part of her was still reeling from the news that Hans was finally going to get rid of his dreadful wife, but that was paling into insignificance because she was reeling from the total change in Marc.

It was as if a different person sat there at the head of the table. Gone was the tight-faced, ill-humoured, short-fused man who could barely hide his constant displeasure and exasperation. Just gone. Now an air of total relaxation radiated from him, with good humour and satisfaction all round…

The difference could not be greater.

Nor the impact it was having on her.

She watched him sit back in his chair, one long leg crossed over the other, completely at his ease.

Was this really Marc Derenz of the frowning brows, the steel jaw, the constant darkling expression in his eyes?

'So,' he said, buttering his brioche, 'what would you like to do now that we have the day to ourselves?'

Tara started. 'What do you mean?' She tried to gather her thoughts. 'Um…if Celine and Hans have gone, I ought to go back to London.'

Suddenly the frown was back again on his face. 'Why?' he demanded.

'Well, I mean… I've done what you brought me out here to do, so there's no point me being here any longer.'

He cut across her. 'Oh, for God's sake—there's no

need to rush off!' He took a breath, his stance altering subtly, as did the expression in his eyes. 'Look, let's just chill, shall we? We damn well deserve it, that's for sure! So, like I say, what would you like to do today?' His eyes rested on her. 'How well do you know the South of France—I mean apart from trailing around the damn shops with Celine and seeing those dire houses she dragged us to? Why don't I show you the South of France that's actually worth seeing?'

He seemed to want an answer, but she could not give one. How could she? This was a Marc Derenz she had never known existed. One who could smile—really smile. One who radiated good humour. Who seemed to be wanting her company for *herself*, not for keeping Celine Neuberger at bay.

She felt something flutter inside her. Something she ought to pay attention to.

'Um… I don't know. I mean…' She looked across at him. His expression was bland and she tried to make it out. 'Why?' she said bluntly. 'As in why do you want me to stay? As what?'

That strange feeling inside her was fluttering again, more strongly now.

'What do you mean, "As what?",' he countered.

'Am I still in your employ, or what? Am I supposed to have some sort of role? Am I—?'

He cut across her questions. 'Tara, don't make this complicated. Stay because you're here…because Celine and Hans have gone…because I want to celebrate their impending divorce. Stay for any damn reason you like!'

He was getting irritated, she could see. For some reason, it made her laugh. 'Oh, that's better,' she said dulcetly. 'I thought the new, improved Marc Derenz was too good to be true!'

For a second he seemed to glower at her. Then his face relaxed. 'You wind me up like no other woman,' he told her.

'You're so easy to wind up,' she said limpidly.

She could feel that flutter inside her getting stronger. Changing her mood. Filling her, suddenly, with a sense of freedom. Of adventure.

He shook his head, that rueful laugh coming again. 'I'm not used to being disagreed with,' he admitted.

Tara's eyes widened. 'No? I'd never have guessed.'

He threw her a look, then lifted both his hands in a gesture of submission. 'Truce time,' he said. He looked at her. 'You know, I'm not really a bear with a sore head most of the time. You've seen me at my worst because of Celine. And,' he admitted, 'you've caught the sharp edge of my ill-humour because of that. But I *can* be nice, you know. Why don't you stick around and find out just how nice, hmm…?'

She felt a hollow inside her, into which a million of the little flutters that had been butterflying inside her suddenly swooped.

Oh, Lord, this was a bad, *bad* idea! To 'stick around', as he'd put it! Yet she wanted to—oh, she wanted to! But on what terms? With what assumptions? That was what she had to get clear. Because otherwise…

She took a breath. 'Marc, these past days have

been…' She tried to find a word to describe them and failed. 'Well, you know—the role-playing. It was…' she swallowed '…confusing.'

She didn't want to recount all the incidents, the memories she couldn't cope with, the times when all self-control had been ripped from her.

He nodded slowly. His dark eyes rested on her with something behind them she did not need a code-breaker to decipher.

'Yes,' he said. 'And it's time—way beyond time— to end that confusion.'

He did not spell it out—he did not have to. She knew that as he went on.

'So let's put the confusion behind us, shall we? And the acting and the role-playing? We'll just take it from here. See what happens.' He paused, those dark eyes unreadable—and yet oh-so-readable. 'What do you say?'

He was waiting for her answer.

She could feel those butterflies swooping around in that hollow space inside her, knew that she'd stopped breathing. Knew why. Knew, as she very slowly exhaled, that whatever she'd said to herself while being so 'confused'—dear God, that word was an under-statement!—about the way this man could make her feel, that now, with just the two of them here, like this, finally free to make their own choices, that she was making a decision that was going to take her to a place with Marc Derenz that she did not know. Had never yet been.

But she wanted to go there with a part of her that

she could not resist. She heard words frame themselves in her mind. Knew them to be true.

It's too late to say no to this—way too late.

As he'd said—no more role-play, no more acting. No more 'confusion'. Just her and Marc…seeing what happened…

And if 'what happened' was her yielding to that oh-so-powerful, never before experienced desire for him, would that really be so bad?

She glanced about her at this beautiful place, at the devastating man sitting there, drawing her so ineluctably. Would it be so bad to experience all that she might with this man? Whatever it brought her?

I've never known a man like this—a man who makes me feel this way. So why should I say no to it? Why not say yes instead…?

She could feel the answer forming in her head, knowing it was the answer she would give him now. A tremor seemed to go through her as slowly she nodded her head.

She saw him smile a smile of satisfaction. Pleased…

His smile widened and he pushed a bowl of pastries towards her. 'Have a croissant,' he invited. 'While we plan our day.'

CHAPTER SEVEN

'So, what do you think?'

Marc slewed the car to a juddering halt at the viewpoint and killed the engine. This was the car he liked to drive when he was at the villa—a low-slung, high-powered beast that snaked up the *corniches*, ate up the road as they gained elevation way up here in the foothills of the Alpes-Maritimes.

He turned to look at the woman sitting beside him in the deep bucket passenger seat as the engine died. Satisfaction filled him. Yes, he had made the right decision. He knew he had—he was definite about it.

The discovery from a clearly upset Hans that morning that he had accepted his marriage was over, and that Celine was not happy with him, had been like a release from prison for Marc. He'd said what needed to be said, organised Hans's flight, then seen him off with a warm handshake.

Celine's departure he had left to his staff while he himself had gone off to phone a jubilant Bernhardt.

And after that there'd only been himself to think about. Basking in heartfelt relief, he'd gone to breakfast in peace, his glance automatically going to the upper balcony. To Tara's bedroom.

Tara.

He had known a decision had to be made.

What am I going to do? Pack her off back to London or...?

Even as he'd framed the question he'd felt the answer blazing in his head. For days now she'd haunted him...that amazing beauty of hers taunting him. His but only in illusion. His only reality, punching through every moment of his time with her, was that he wanted to say to hell with the role he'd hired her to play. He wanted *more*.

And when she'd walked out onto the terrace he'd taken one look at her and made his decision.

No, she wasn't from his world. And, had it not been for the insufferable Celine and his need to keep her away from him, he'd never have let Tara get anywhere near him. Yes, he was breaking all his rules never to get involved with someone like her.

And he just did not care.

Not any more.

I want her—and for whatever time we have together it will be good. I know that for absolute sure—

It was good already. Good to have had that relaxed, leisurely breakfast, deciding how to spend their day—a day to themselves, a day to enjoy. Good to have her sitting beside him now, her sandaled feet stretched out in the capacious footwell, wearing a casual top and skinny cotton leggings that hugged those fantastic legs of hers. Her hair was caught back with a barrette and her make-up was minimal. But her beauty didn't need make-up.

His eyes rested on her now, drinking her in.

'The view is fabulous,' she was exclaiming. Then she frowned. 'It's just a pity it's so built up all along the coastline.'

Marc nodded. 'Yes, it's a victim of overdevelopment. Which is why I like being out on the Cap—it's more like the Riviera was before the war, when the villa was built.'

He gunned the engine again, to start their descent, telling her how the villa had been party central in the days of his great-grandfather.

It was a subject he continued over lunch, stopping off at a little *auberge* that he liked to go to when he wanted to get away from his usual plush lifestyle.

'He invited everyone who was anyone—painters, ex-pat Americans, film-makers, novelists.'

'It sounds very glamorous.' Tara smiled as he regaled her with stories.

'My grandfather was much quieter in temperament— and my father too. When I was a boy we spent the summers here. Hans and his first wife and their children were often visitors, before my parents were killed—'

He broke off, aware that he was touching on something he did not usually talk about to the women in his life. But Tara was looking at him, the light of sympathy in her eyes.

'Killed?' she echoed.

'They both died in a helicopter crash when I was twenty-three,' he said starkly.

Her expression of sympathy deepened. 'That must have been so hard for you.'

His mouth tightened. 'Yes,' was all he said. All he could say.

He watched her take a slow forkful of food, then she looked at him again. 'It can't compare, I know, but I have some idea of what you went through.' She paused. 'My parents are both in the army, and part of me is always waiting to hear that…well, that they aren't going to come home again. That kind of fear is always there, at some level.'

It came to him that he knew very little about this woman. He only knew the surface, that fabulous beauty of hers that so took his breath away.

'Did you—what is that old-fashioned phrase in English?—"follow the drum"?' he heard himself asking.

She shook her head. 'No, I was sent to boarding school at eight, and spent most of my holidays with my grandparents. Oh, I flew out to see my parents from time to time, and they came home on leave sometimes, but I didn't see a great deal of them when I was growing up. I still don't, really. We get on perfectly well, but I guess we're quite remote from one another in a way.'

He took a mouthful of wine. It was only a *vin de table*, made from the landlord's own grapes, but it went well with the simple fare they were eating. He found himself wondering whether Tara would have preferred a more expensive restaurant, but she seemed content enough.

She was relaxing more all the time, he could tell. It was strange to be with her on her own, without Celine and Hans to distort things. Strange and…

Good. It's good to be here with her. Getting to know her.

And why not? She came from a different world, and that was refreshing in itself. But it was about himself that he heard himself speaking next.

'I was very close to my parents,' he said. 'Which made it so hard when—' He broke off. Took another mouthful of wine. 'Hans was very kind—he stepped in, got me through it. He stood by me and his wife did too. I was…shell-shocked.' He frowned, not looking at her, but back into that nightmare time all those years ago. 'Hans helped me with the bank too. Not everyone on the board thought I could cope at so young an age. He guided me, advised me—made sure I took control of everything.'

'No wonder,' she said carefully, 'you're so loyal to him now.'

His eyes went to hers. 'Yes,' he said simply.

She smiled. 'Well, I hope his life will soon be a lot happier.' Her expression changed, softened. 'He's such a lovely man—it's so sad that he was widowed. Do you think he'll marry again eventually? I mean, someone *not* like Celine!'

'It would be good for him, I think,' Marc agreed. 'But, as I said to you, the trouble is he can be too kind-hearted for his own good—easy for him to be taken advantage of by an ambitious female.'

'Yes…' She nodded. 'He needs someone *much* nicer than Celine! Someone,' she mused, 'who really values him. And…' she gave a wry smile '…who enjoys German romantic poetry!'

Marc pushed his empty plate aside, wanting to change the subject. Of course he was glad for Hans that he'd freed himself from Celine's talons, but right now the only person he wanted to think about was Tara.

She had already finished her *plat du jour*, and she smiled at him as she reached for a crusty slice of baguette from the woven basket sitting on the chequered tablecloth.

'You've no idea how good it is to simply eat French bread!' she told him feelingly. 'Or that croissant I had at breakfast! So many models are on starvation diets—it's horrendous!'

He watched her busy herself, mopping up the last of the delicious homemade sauce on her empty plate, disposing of it with relish.

'Won't you have to starve extra to atone for this now?' he posed, a smile in his voice.

She shook her head. 'Nope. I'm going to be chucking in the modelling lark. It's been good to me, I can't deny that, but I haven't done anything since university that qualifies me for any other particular career— not that I want to work nine-to-five anyway. I've got other plans. In fact,' she added, 'it's thanks to being out here that I can make them real now.'

He started to ask what they were, but the owner of the *auberge* was approaching, asking what else they might like. They ordered cheese and coffee, changing the subject to what they would do in the afternoon. It was an easy conversation, relaxed and convivial.

Marc's eyes rested on her as they discussed what she might like to see. She was so different, he observed. That all too familiar argumentative antagonism was gone, that back-talking that had irritated him so much. Oh, from time to time there was a wicked gleam in her eye when she said something he knew was designed to try and wind him up, but his own mood was now so totally different it had no effect except to make him laugh.

She's easy to be with.

It was a strange thing to think about her after all the aggro, all the tension that had been between them.

We've both lightened up, he mused.

Only one area was generating any tension between them now. But it was at a low level, like a current of electricity running constantly between them, visible only in sudden veiled glances, in the casual brush of hands, in body contact that was not intentional or was simply necessary, such as handing her a menu, helping her back into the low-slung car as they set off again, catching the light floral fragrance of her scent.

His eyes wanted to linger on her rather than on the road twisting ahead. On their constant mutual awareness of each other. He let it run—low voltage, but there. This was not the time or the occasion to do anything about it. That was for later…for this evening. And then… Ah, then… He smiled inwardly, feeling sensual anticipation ease through him. Then he would give it free rein. And discover, to the full, all that he burned to find in her.

There would be no more drawing back—no more hauling himself away, castigating himself for his loss of self-control, no more anger at himself for wanting her so much…

I am simply not going to fight it any more.

He had not deliberately sought her out, or selected her for a relationship. She had come into his life almost accidentally, certainly unintentionally, because of his urgent need to protect himself from Hans's amoral wife—but she was here now. And after all he'd had to put up with over Celine, damn it, he deserved a reward!

He glanced sideways at her as they drove back down towards the coast. And she deserved something good too, didn't she? She'd done the job he'd set her—triumphantly!—so why shouldn't he make sure that now she had as enjoyable a time remaining as he could ensure?

He would do his best, his very best, to ensure that. It was impossible for her to deny the desire that flared between them, and now there was no more aggravation, no more frustration, no more confusion, no more role-playing and no more barriers.

As his eyes went back to the twisting road ahead, and he steered his powerful car round the hairpin bends, he felt his blood heat pleasurably in his veins.

Whatever the risks of breaking the rules he lived his life by—Tara would be worth it.

Most definitely worth it...

Tara sat at the silvered Art Deco dressing table, carefully applying minimal eye make-up—just a touch of mascara tonight was all that was needed—and a sheen of lip gloss. Her mood was strange. Everything was so similar to the previous night, when she'd been making up her face and getting dressed for that yacht party with Celine's awful friends, and yet everything was totally different.

Marc was different.

That was the key to it, she knew. That 'bear with a sore head', as he had called himself with total accuracy, was simply gone. She couldn't help but make a face at how he'd railed at her. This time yesterday he'd laid into her furiously in this very room for daring to take matters into her own hands, and to damn well lay off him! But her ploy had worked—and he'd had to admit it had worked even better than either of them could have imagined!

And now, mission more than accomplished, they could both have their reward for freeing poor Hans from his ghastly wife.

Reward...

The word hovered in Tara's head. Beguiling, tempting.

She knew just what that reward was going to be...

Impossible not to know...

And to know with a certainty that had been building up in her hour after hour, all day.

Marc was right—whatever was happening between them, it was powerful and irresistible. They wanted each other—had done since first seeing each other, and had gone on wanting each other all through those torturous days when they'd both been forced to pretend in public what they had tried so hopelessly to deny in private.

They wanted each other. It was the one undeniable truth between them.

It was as simple as that.

Her eyes flickered around the beautiful room and she looked out through the windows to the darkening view beyond, over the gardens and the sea. Her very first thought on arrival here had been how gorgeous it all was, and how she should make the most of it.

Well…a half-smile played around her mouth…now she *was* going to make the most of it. And of the man who came with it.

The man who, even when he was at his most overbearing, his most obnoxious, his most short-tempered, possessed the ability to set her pulse racing, her blood surging, her heart-rate quickening…

She could feel it now, and with another little flutter inside her, she got to her feet.

I can't resist him and there's no reason to. He wants me—I want him. I know it won't last—can't last—but I must simply enjoy this time with him.

He wasn't a man she'd ever have got involved with had it not been for him hiring her, but since he had, and she was—well, why not accept what was happening between them?

Why not—as she was doing now—slip into an ankle-length, fine cotton sundress in a vivid floral print of vibrant blues and crimsons that was nothing like the formal evening gowns and cocktail dresses she'd worn when the Neubergers were there. She was 'off duty' now, and she wanted only to feel comfortable.

It was a look that Marc had echoed, she saw as she joined him out on the terrace. He wore a plain white open-necked shirt with the cuffs turned back and dark blue chinos. Still devastatingly attractive, but relaxed.

The two of them were all set, ready for a comfortable and relaxed evening together...

She felt that little flutter inside her again.

But that was for later. For now there was just the warmth in Marc's eyes—a warmth that wasn't only male appreciation of her, but a side of him she hadn't seen in him before, except for when he had greeted Hans. A side of him that had so taken her aback as he'd dropped that perpetual ill-humour of his.

He was walking towards her, an open bottle of champagne and two flutes in his hands. He set the flutes on a table laid for dinner, with candles glowing in protective glass cases, and started to pour the champagne. Silently he handed her a softly effervescing glass, keeping the other for himself.

'It's a champagne evening,' he announced, a smile playing at his mouth. He raised his glass. 'To us,' he said softly, his eyes never leaving her. 'To our champagne evening. *Salut!*'

And it *was* a salute, Tara knew. It was a recognition of what was happening between them—what had been happening ever since their first encounter. An acknowledgement that neither of them could walk away now from the other…from this champagne evening.

I want this—I want everything about it. Even for the short while that it will be mine…

The words were in her head—unstoppable. And she didn't want to stop them, to silence them. All she wanted, on this evening of all evenings, was what there was and what there was to come.

'*Salut…*' she said in soft reply, and took a mouthful of the delicate drink, her eyes still holding his. There was a glow in her body, a sweetness in her veins, a low pulse at her throat.

He drank as well, and then, with a smile, said, 'Walk with me.'

She did, and they strolled across the darkening garden to the edge of the lawn, where the manicured grass gave way to rougher land, and then a rocky shore tumbled down to the lapping sea below.

There was a little jetty, and steps cut into the rocky outcrop to take them there, and he led her down. They stood on the jetty awhile, looking out across the night-filled sea. From this point at the tip of the Cap there was no line of sight to the shoreline with all its bright lights. Even the villa behind them was not visible this low below the shoreline.

'We might be on a desert island…' Tara breathed, her voice still soft. 'All on our own.'

At her side, Marc gave a low laugh. 'The world vanished away,' he said.

He turned to her. Lifted the hand that was not holding his flute to trail a finger along the contours of her mouth.

'I want this time with you,' he said, and she could hear the husk in his voice now, feel the frisson in her veins that it engendered. 'We are free to have it—and I very much wish to share it with you.'

There was a question in his voice—and yet an answer too. For how could she refuse him? She knew she would not be here, standing with him out on the jetty, beneath the gathering night, if she did not want what he wanted too.

Marc felt desire creaming inside him, yet he knew he must not be precipitate. He had considered her out of bounds, was breaking all his rules by indulging himself with her, and as that was so he wanted to take from this forbidden *liaison d'amour* all that it could offer him.

And it will be worth it! She is promising everything I want—everything I have already so tantalisingly tasted.

Tara made no reply to what he had said, but she did not need to, she knew. Perhaps, it was unwise, letting herself be drawn into a world that was not hers, to a man who could never be hers for that reason, and she knew it must be brief, but she accepted it. Accepted all of it. This beautiful villa, this beautiful place, and the man whose domain it was.

She took another slow mouthful of her champagne, feeling its potency ease into her bloodstream, committing her to what she was doing.

They stood awhile, as the sky darkened to absolute night and one by one the stars began to shine. The low lapping of the water was seductive…as seductive as the warm, caressing breeze that lifted off the sea. Then, the sky dark, the champagne drunk, they made their way back to the terrace to dine together.

What they ate Tara would not afterwards remember. She knew only that it was delicious, and that the conversation flowed between them as effortlessly now as it had been fraught before. Had they really been so…so intemperate towards each other? So antagonistic, so irritated and exasperated by each other? It seemed impossible. Impossible to think of Marc as the man he had been when now his ready smile, his low laugh, his lambent eyes were warm upon her.

What they talked about she would not remember either. She only knew that another conversation was taking place as well—a conversation that, as the meal ended and liqueurs were consumed, the coffee pot drained, he suddenly brought to vivid life as he reached for her hand, drew her to her feet.

The staff were long gone, and they were here alone on the candlelit terrace. He stood in front of her, so dark against the night beyond. She caught his scent, felt herself sway and smile…

He said her name—a caress—and lifted his hand to her hair to draw her closer to him. But there was no need. With a little sigh, closing her eyelids, she let her body fold against his, let it rest, as it wanted so much to do, against the strong column of his. He took her weight against him effortlessly and her hand slid around his waist, resting on the cool leather of his belt, the tips of her fingers feeling the hard heat of his flesh beneath the thin fabric of his shirt.

She gave a soft, almost inaudible sigh in her throat. And then his mouth was silencing her. Moving with the velvet softness that had caused her sleepless nights, and which now sent a drowning bliss through her with every feathering touch.

She gave herself to it. This time… Ah, this time there was no barrier, no regret, no resistance to what was happening between them. She was giving herself utterly to it…

Their kiss was long, unhurried, for they had all the night before them… Then, as her breasts engorged, their peaks cresting against the hard wall of his muscled chest, she heard him growl, felt his mouth releasing hers. His eyes poured down into hers, and she felt with a frisson of arousal that he was responding as strongly as was she.

Was it wickedness that made her loop her hands around his neck and whisper, 'Shall we slow dance?'

For tonight they could—oh, yes, they could indeed—and with that came the knowledge that now there need be no more play-acting, that they could finally accept and revel in the desire that flamed between them. No more being thwarted, no more pulling away... At last they could give in to what they had wanted from the very first.

The growl came again—a low rasp—and instead of an answer she was suddenly, breathlessly, swept up into his arms.

'We can do better than that,' he told her, and the deep husk in his voice was telling her just what that 'better' was going to be.

She gave a half-cry, half-laugh, and then he was striding indoors, across the marble hall, up the marble stairs. She clung to him, and she was held fast in his powerful grip as he carried her along the landing, to head inside a room she had never yet stepped into.

It was dark, but he knew the way. Knew the way to the wide bed waiting for them. And as he lowered her to its surface, coming down beside her, he knew there were no more questions to ask, no more answers. Their bodies had asked and answered all that was needed.

Desire—that was the question *and* the answer. And it flamed between them, powerful and unquenchable. They were to be aroused by all that it could offer, to savour it...to enjoy. In a sharing of slow, caressing pleasure, a banquet of the senses.

He leant over, dark against the dimness of the room, smoothing the tumbled mass of her glorious hair, spearing his fingers through the lush tresses as she gazed up at him, starlight from the undrawn drapes shining in her dilated eyes. Waiting for his possession. For her possession of him.

He kissed her again slowly, tasting, drawing from her every drop of nectar. Again he felt his body fill with desire, with wanting.

For a moment he held back, as if to give himself one last chance to draw away completely, but she caught his mouth again, arching her neck, her spine, putting her hands around his back, drawing him down to her to feel the swell of her breasts, to hear the soft moan of desire in her throat.

He gave a low, husky laugh, cut short as his kiss deepened, his arousal surged. His palm closed over one peak and her soft moan came again as she pressed against his caressing hand, wanting only what he could arouse in her. Heat filled her body—her limbs…the soft vee of her thighs.

Her dress was in the way, and restlessly she sought to free herself. But he was there before her. His hands slipped the material from her, cast it aside even as he cast aside his own clothing, freeing them both to come together now, as their bodies longed to do, with a will they could not stop, nor wanted to.

They wanted only to do as they were doing—to wind themselves around each other, pinioning and clasping. His mouth was gliding down the satin contours of her slender body, and again low moans came from her.

Her head twisted helplessly on the pillow as she gave herself to his silken touch. Desire soared within her and she wanted more—oh, she wanted all of him! She felt her thighs slacken, her body's heat flare, and her fingers clawed over his strong, muscled shoulders.

She drew him into her and he surged in full possession. She cried out, gasping at the power of him, the potency. Her hands clutched him tighter, and more tightly yet, as he moved on her, within her, releasing with every surge more and more of what was rising within her, unstoppable, unquenchable. A glory of sensation, a gasping of delight, of mounting urgency…

And then it broke within her, flooding out into every vein, every portion of her body, racing out from her pulsing core to the furthest extremity, her whole body burning in this furnace of ecstasy.

As she cried out he surged within her again, his body thrashing, fusing with hers like metal melting into metal, white-hot and searing.

And she was everything he desired—everything he wanted. She was fulfilling all her promise, pulsing around his body, her own body afire, until the fire consumed itself and he felt her hands at his shoulders slacken, felt her whole body slacken.

He felt his do so too, heavy now upon her, and he rolled her, with the last of his strength, so that she was beside him and he could fold her to him, feel her shuddering body calm, her racing heartbeat slow, her hectic breathing quieten. He held her as his own slugging heart steadied, his limbs heavy, inert.

Slowly he felt the lassitude of her body's repletion ease through her as he stroked her hair, murmuring to her he knew not what. He knew only that his soft caressing, his softer murmurs, brought her to stillness in his cradling arms.

He felt his eyelids droop, sleep rushing upon him. He knew he must yield to it—for now. But as consciousness slipped from him, and the warmth and the silken length of her body pressed against his, something told him his sleep would not be long...

Nor hers...

CHAPTER EIGHT

MORNING LIGHT WAS bathing them. Tara could feel it warm upon her back, which was partly covered by a single sheet. Her arm was flung across the bare torso of the man beside her, still asleep.

She herself was still drowsy and somnolent from the night that had passed. A night like no other she had ever known.

Memory drenched through her and she hugged her naked body more closely against the one she was entwined with. Had she ever imagined a night like that was possible?

Time and time again he had possessed her—each time a consummation of bliss that had caused her to cry out over and over again as her body had burned with his, in a heat that had been a consuming fire, bathing their straining muscles and sated flesh, her spine arched like a bowstring, his body plunging into hers, her hands clutching at the twisting contours of his shoulders, her head thrashing on the pillow as they reached their peaks together.

And then peace had blanketed down upon her,

upon them both—an exhaustion, a sweeping sigh of exhalation as their bodies had closed upon each other, no space between them, pressed to each other in heated fastness, hers turned into his, folded against him, her limbs heavy, his yet heavier. And then, dazed and dazzled, she had sought the rest that had come—instant and obliterating.

Only for him to rouse her yet again…and for her to wake in an instant, to overpowering desire again…

Memories indeed…

She felt her mouth smile against his throat, her eyelids flutter, felt him stir in answer, his hand easing across her flank with soft caress.

For a while they simply lay there, letting the sun from the windows warm their entwined bodies, dozing and then waking slowly to full awareness of the day. Saying nothing, for there was no need.

Not until Marc, with a stretching of his limbs, turned his head to smile across at her. 'Breakfast? Or—?'

She laid a finger across his mouth. 'Breakfast!' she said, shaking her head. 'One night with you lasts a long, *long* time…'

He gave a laugh, pleased with her answer. Pleased with the entire universe. He had known women before—many women. But this one…

His mind sheered away. It wasn't necessary to think, to examine or analyse. It was only necessary to enjoy this gloriously sunny morning, here in the place he loved where he never seemed to have enough time to spend. It was only necessary to get himself up from his bed, reach for a grey silk robe and knot it around his waist.

His muscles felt stretched, fully used...

He reached a hand down to her. 'If you want breakfast,' he said, and there was a husk in his voice with which Tara had become very familiar with in the long, sensual reaches of the night, 'you had better use your own shower.'

He nodded towards the communicating door, then headed for his own en suite bathroom. At the door to it he turned. She was starting to stand up, and the sight of her fabulous racehorse body, full in the sunlight now, almost made him change his mind and carry her through to his own shower, where washing was *not* going to be a priority...

But his stomach gave a low grumble. He had expended a great deal of energy last night and it needed to be replenished.

So he said only, 'See you downstairs. And think about what you would like to do today—because if you can't come up with anything I have a very enticing idea of my own...'

He let his voice trail off and raised a hand in half-salute, leaving her to her own rising.

When they regrouped, out on the terrace, he threw himself into a chair. He was wearing shorts, and a striped top.

Tara, settling herself down opposite him, gave a laugh. 'You look like a *matelot*!' She smiled.

Marc's eyes glinted. 'The very thing,' he said. He

sat back. 'It's a beautiful day and the wind is just right—let's take to the water.'

She laughed. 'Is *that* your enticing idea?' she returned. 'I was assuming something far more...*physical*...' she said wickedly.

'Depends where we drop anchor,' Marc returned, his expression deadpan.

She laughed again. She could have laughed at anything this morning—this glorious, *glorious* morning. The morning after the night before...and the night before had been like no other night had ever been...

Could ever be...

For just a moment she felt a dart pierce her. Would anything in all her life ever compare to the night she'd spent in the arms of this man she had so rashly committed herself to? A man she knew she should never have given herself to but had simply not been able to resist?

What if nothing could?

She pushed the question aside. This was not a morning for questions—for doubts of any kind. She was having this time with Marc, and if he was a million miles from her own normality—well, so be it. Too late for regrets now, even if she wanted to have them—which, right now, she did *not*.

She reached for a croissant, revelling in its yeasty temptation, in yielding to *all* temptations. 'That sounds fun.' She smiled. 'I didn't see a boat moored at the jetty, though.'

'It's kept at the dock in Pierre-les-Pins, at the head of the bay. I'm having it sailed to the jetty now.'

He said it casually, but the remark lingered in Tara's head as she busied herself with her breakfast. It was another reminder of just how hugely wealthy he was. Just as much as this villa was a reminder, with its manicured lawn and pool, and its complement of attentive staff, and the top-marque car he'd driven her about in yesterday, and the chauffeur-driven limo, the gourmet restaurants, and the designer wardrobe he'd snapped his fingers for, and every other element of his life.

Unease filtered through her. Before, while she'd been working for him, it hadn't bothered her, his vast wealth. But now… Was she wise to get personally involved with him in any way? Even for what must inevitably be only a brief time, in this mutually self-indulgent 'reward' for their torturous past week? With a man from a world so entirely different from her own?

It was difficult to remember that—to believe in all that fabulous wealth of his, in the bank that bore his name and was the source of all that wealth—when she was skimming over the azure waters of the Mediterranean, the breeze filling the billowing sails.

But the huge disparity in their wealth was harder to ignore that evening when, gowned once more in one of the fabulous couture evening dresses supplied for her by him for the role that was no longer a role, but real, for whatever short duration it would prove, he whisked her off in the sleek, chauffeured car, to dine out in another fearsomely expensive Michelin-starred restaurant, where every dish cost a fortune and the wines ten times as much.

She put it aside. For this evening, this time they would have together, it was just the two of them, lovers for real now. She felt a little shimmer of wonder at the transformation. She could actually enjoy it. She had Marc to herself, and it was 'new Marc'—Marc with his ready smile, his air of absolute relaxation, total well-being.

He raised his glass to her and she did likewise, taking a sip of the formidably pricey vintage wine, savouring it even as she savoured all the wonderful delicacies on offer from the menu.

'This is beyond heaven!' She sighed blissfully as whatever concoction he'd ordered for her slipped down her throat. 'I could really get used to this! How on earth am I going to go back to my usual humble fare after this?'

She expected to hear his low laugh, which she was getting used to hearing now, but it didn't come. Instead there was a flickering in his eyes, as if his thoughts were suddenly elsewhere. And in a place he did not care for.

She wondered at it, then set it aside. Nothing was going to spoil this evening. She gazed around the restaurant, taking it in, knowing that this was an experience she must make the most of. Once she was in her little cottage in Dorset, places like this would be a distant memory only.

A little pang went through her and her eyes moved back to the man sitting opposite her. He, too, one day, would be only a distant memory...

There was a tiny catch in her throat and she reached

for her wine glass, made some deliberately light re-mark, to which Marc responded this time—as if he, too, had set aside something there was no point think-ing about. Not now…not tonight. Not with the night ahead of them…

Anticipation thrummed through her, and a sud-den sensual awareness. Her eyes went to him across the table, caught his, saw in them what she knew was in hers… What remained in them all through their long, leisurely and exquisite meal, as conversation flowed between them—easy now, when it had been impossible before.

It was nearly midnight before they left—but when they returned to the villa Tara discovered that the night was still young…

Their night lasted till dawn crept over the edge of the world, and brought with its first light the sleep her body was too exhausted to deny… The sleep that overtook their bodies, all passion finally spent, folded around each other as if parting could never come.

It was a false illusion…

Marc was in his office, attempting to catch up with work. But his mind wasn't on it. He gave a rueful grimace. Where his mind was right now was out by the pool—the pool beside which Tara would be sun-ning herself, turning her silken skin a deeper shade of delectable gold, all the more enticing to caress…

With a groan, he tore the seductive vision from his head and focussed on the computer screen, on the myriad complexities of his normal working life making their usual round-the-clock demands on him. Demands that he had no inclination to meet at the moment but that were piling up nevertheless.

He knew he could not postpone them indefinitely. That at some point he'd have to knuckle down and deal with them. The truth was, he wasn't used to taking so much time out from work.

Work had dominated his life ever since he'd had to shoulder all the responsibilities of his inheritance at a painfully early age. Even when he set aside his workload for social engagements, or for his carefully considered forays into highly selective affairs, as was his habit, they never interfered with his primary task in life—to see Banc Derenz through to the next era of its survival in an ever-changing financial landscape. So why, he pondered now frowningly, the figures on the screen ignored still, was he being so careless of his responsibilities at this time?

At first he'd put his indulgence at giving in to his inconveniently overpowering attraction to Tara simply as relief at getting the wretched Celine off his case once and for all. But that had been two weeks ago—two weeks of pure self-indulgence, as he was well aware. Of indulging himself with Tara—giving himself to a sensual feast and to a time out of his customary highly disciplined and demanding lifestyle to simply…simply what?

To have a holiday.

That was what he was doing. Simply having a holiday with this irresistible woman! A holiday that was an endless drift of golden days here in the balmy weather of the Riviera. Lounging by the pool, taking out the sailboat, driving along the coast or up into the hills, making a foray across the border into Italy one day to explore San Remo, strolling around the perfumeries of Grasse another day, heading further still to St Raphael, with its ochre-red cliffs, and then St Tropez, with all the nostalgia of its fashionable heyday in the sixties. They had explored the villages and landscapes that had so beguiled the Impressionists, wandered around the narrow streets of the old town in Nice, strolled along the seafront in Cannes, lunched on one of the many private beaches, or out on the jetty over the water...

A procession of easy-going days, relaxed and carefree, before returning home to the villa...and all the sensual delights of the nights they shared.

He shifted in his seat. When would he tire of Tara? When would her allure grow stale? When would he not want to trouble himself with making conversation with her, engaging in repartee as she presumed to tease him and he returned as good as he got, volleying with her until they both were laughing...or kissing...

I must tire of her soon. Surely I must?

She wasn't from his world, so how could he think of her as anything other than a passing *amour*? Oh, she'd adapted to it easily enough—but then, what woman *wouldn't* find it easy to adapt to the wealthy ease of his highly privileged life.

Has she adapted too well? Got too used to it?

The thought was in his head before he could stop it. Reminding him of all the reasons why he never took up with women who did not share his own life-style in their own financial right.

His eyes went to his screen. No sum of money there was without a whole string of zeroes after it—it was the realm he worked in, that encompassed the accounts of his extremely rich clients. Sums of money that the likes of Tara would never see in her lifetime...

Memory scraped in his head. Unwelcome, but intruding all the same. How Tara had sat with Celine on that ultra-tedious afternoon in Monte Carlo, and made that casual comment that 'marrying money' was still a sure-fire way to help oneself to riches. He'd considered it a snipe at Celine, but now, his frown came again. But maybe it was something she believed herself?

More memories came...uglier and more intrusive, forcing their way in. Marianne...making up to him... enticing him and luring him, the young heir to Banc Derenz, only to callously abandon him for a much safer financial bet—a man with his own wealth already safely in his pockets.

Another image formed in his mind. Sitting in that restaurant with Tara—one of the most exclusive and expensive on the Riviera—the day after their first night together. *'I could really get used to this!'* she'd said, and sighed pleasurably...

More thoughts came to him—disturbing and uneasy. He had declared to Celine that Tara was his fiancée, and the sole purpose of the announcement had been to try and get Hans's wife's clutching claws off him. But had that impulsive proposal set thoughts running in Tara's head? Was she remembering them when they were together now? When they kissed... embraced...made love?

Does she think I might propose for real? Make her my wife?

Roughly, he pushed his chair away from his desk. He would not let such thoughts in. He glanced at his watch. She'd been sunning herself far too long—she must not burn her skin...her oh-so-delectable skin.

Again memory skimmed in his mind—of how irritated he'd been that first day here, to arrive and find the woman he had hired to keep Celine at bay behaving as if she were here on a free luxury holiday.

Well, now she really is here on a free luxury holiday...

Again the unwelcome thought was in his head. Again he dismissed it. For she could enjoy this time with him with his blessing—enjoy all the luxury he took for granted himself. His expression changed. After all, *she* was a luxury herself—to him. An indulgence like none he'd ever experienced. And he wanted to indulge himself...

An anticipatory smile played about his mouth. Her heated skin would need cooling down—and a shower together was the very thing to achieve that. He would lather her body all over with his own hands...every beautiful centimetre of her...

His mood much improved, he abandoned any fruitless attempt to work and strode impatiently from the room to make his anticipation reality.

* * *

Tara stretched languorously and rolled over so that it was her back—bare from neck to hip—that received the blessing of the sun's rays.

This really was *gorgeous.* To be basking here in the sun, after a late, leisurely breakfast, with nothing more strenuous to do than maybe take a cooling dip in the pool beside her and then, later on, drape herself in her chiffon sarong and drift across to where the staff were setting out their customary al fresco lunch.

She and Marc would make their *déjeuner* of the finest delicacies, all freshly prepared by hands other than theirs, and whisked away at the end of their meal by those other hands, leaving them nothing to do but laze the afternoon away or take the sailboat out, or swim off the jetty in the calm seas lapping the shore. Or maybe, if they were feeling energetic, head off in that powerful black beast of a car, purring like a contented tiger, to see yet more of the fabled Côte d'Azur.

And then they'd return as the sun was lowering, to sip sundowners by the pool and wait for yet another gourmet meal to be served to them by others' labour.

A pampered lifestyle indeed...

Idly she flexed her toes, eased the arms cushioning her head, utterly at ease. *I could get used to this*...

Oh, she could indeed! she thought, half-ruefully, half-languorously. No wonder the rich liked being rich...

But, for all the luxury of her surroundings and the ease of her days, she knew that not a single glass of vintage champagne, not a moment spent lounging like this beside the pool, would count for anything at all were she not here with Marc.

It was Marc and Marc alone who was turning this luxury into paradise for her. Marc—who only had to glance at her with those dark, knowing eyes of his and she would feel her whole body flicker as if with unseen electricity. All he had to do was touch her…

A shadow fell over her, and as if she'd conjured him from her thoughts he was hunkering down beside her, letting his index finger stroke sensuously down the long curve of her spine, arousing every bit of that flickering electricity.

She gave a little moan in her throat at the sensation and heard his low laugh. Then, suddenly, she was being caught in his arms, dizzyingly swept up. Her moan of sensuous pleasure turned into a squeal, and he laughed again.

'Time for a cool-down,' he informed her.

For a second she thought he was going to toss her into the pool, but he was striding indoors with her, heading upstairs. Suddenly mindful of her abandoned bikini top, she pressed herself hurriedly against his torso, lest they encounter one of the staff. She felt her breasts crest, and knew there was only one way that this was going to end…

Lunch was going to have to wait…

'What's the plan for this afternoon?' Tara enquired casually as, quite some time later, they settled down to the delicious *al fresco* lunch awaiting them on the vine-shaded terrace.

'What would you like to do?' Marc asked indulgently.

His mood was good—very good. Their refreshing shower had done a lot more than refresh him…

Have I ever known a woman like her?

The question played in his mind and he let it. So did the answer. But the answer was one that, unlike the question, he suddenly did not care to consider. Did he really want to accept that no other woman in his life had come anywhere close to how Tara made him feel? Accept how she could elicit his desire for her simply by glancing at him with those amazing blue-green eyes?

How long had this idyll here at the villa been so far? A fortnight? Longer still? The days were slipping by like pearls on a necklace…he'd given up counting them. He did not wish to count them. Did not wish to remember time, the days, the month progressing. He liked this timeless drift of day after day after day…

'You choose,' Tara said lazily, helping herself to some oozing Camembert, lavishing it on fresh crusty bread.

She must have put on pounds, she thought idly, but the thought did not trouble her. She didn't care. Didn't even want to think about going back to London, picking up on the last of her modelling assignments, giving notice on the flat-share, clearing her things and heading west to move into her thatched cottage and start the life she had planned for so long.

It seemed a long, long way away from here. From now.

Her eyes went to Marc, her gaze softening, just

drinking him in as he helped himself to salad, poured mineral water for them both...

He caught her looking at him and his expression changed. 'Don't look at me like that...' There was the familiar husk in his voice.

She gave a small laugh. 'I haven't the strength for anything else but looking,' she said. Her voice lowered. 'And looking at you is all I want to do...just to gaze and gaze upon your manly perfection!'

There was a lazy teasing in her voice and his mouth twitched. He let his own gaze rest on her—on her feminine perfection...

Dimly, he became aware that his phone was ringing. Usually he put it on to silent, but he must have flicked it on when he'd attempted—so uselessly—to knuckle down to some work.

He glanced at it irately. He didn't want to be disturbed. When he saw the identity of the caller his irritation mounted. He picked up the phone. He might as well answer and get it over and done with...

Nodding his apologies to Tara, he went indoors. Disappeared inside his study. Behind him, at the table, Tara tucked in, unconcerned, turning her mind to how they might amuse themselves that afternoon.

But into her head came threads of thoughts she didn't want to let in. She might not want the time to pass, but it was passing all the same. How long ago had she flown out here from London? It plucked at her mind that she should check her diary—see when she had to be back there, get in touch with her booker. Show her face again...

I don't want to!

The protest was in her head, and it was nothing to do with her wanting to quit modelling and escape to her cottage. It was deeper than that—stronger. More disturbing.

I don't want this time with Marc to end.

That was the blunt truth of it. But end it must— how could it not? How could it *possibly* not? How could anything come of this beyond what they had here and now—this lotus-eating idyll of lazy days and sensual nights…?

She shifted restlessly in her chair, wanting Marc to come back. Wanting her eyes to light upon him and him to smile, to resume their discussion about how to spend a lazy afternoon together…

But when he did walk out, only a handful of moments later, it was not relief that she felt when her eyes went to him. Not relief at all…

She'd wondered when this idyll would end. Well, she had her answer now, in the grim expression on Marc's face—an expression she had not seen since before the routing of Celine. It could presage nothing but ill.

She heard him speak, his voice terse.

'I'm sorry, I'm going to have to leave for New York. Something's come up that I can't avoid.' He took a breath, throwing himself into his chair. 'One of my clients—one of the bank's very wealthiest— wants to bring forward the date of his annual review. I always attend in person, and it's impossible for me to get out of it. Damned nuisance though it is!'

Tara looked at him. She kept her face carefully blank. 'When…when do you have to leave?' she asked.

'Tomorrow. I should really leave today, but…'

'Oh,' she said. It seemed, she thought, an inadequate thing to say. But the words she wanted to say, to cry out to him, she could not. *Should* not.

I don't want this time to end! Not yet!

Even as she heard the cry inside her head she knew it should not be there. Knew she should not be feeling what she was feeling now—as if she were being hollowed out from the inside. She had no right to feel that way.

Right from the start she had known that whatever it was she was going to indulge herself in with Marc, it was only that—an indulgence. They had come together only by circumstance, nothing more. Nothing had ever been intended to happen between them.

He never meant to have this time with me. Would never have chosen it freely. It was simply because of his need to use me to keep Celine away from him! He'd never have looked twice at me otherwise—not with any intent of making something of it.

Memory, harsh and undeniable, sprang into her head. Of the way Marc had stood there, that first day she'd arrived, telling her that her presence was just a job, that he was out of bounds to her, that she was there only to play-act and she was not to think otherwise. He could not have spelt out more clearly, more brutally, that she wasn't a woman he would choose for a romance, an affair, any relationship at all…

She knew it. Accepted it. Had no choice but to accept it. But even as she told herself she could hear other words crying out in her head.

He might ask me to go with him! He might—he could! He could say to me just casually, easily, Come to New York with me—let me show you the sights. Be with me there.

She looked at him now. His expression was remote. He was thinking about things other than her. Not asking her to go with him.

Then, abruptly, his eyes met hers. Veiled. He picked up his discarded napkin, resumed his meal. 'So,' he said, and his voice was nothing different from what it always was, 'if this is to be our last day, how would you like to spend it?'

She felt that hollow widening inside her. But she knew that all she could do was echo his light tone, though she could feel her fingers clenching on her knife and fork as she, too, resumed eating.

'Can we just stay here, at the villa?' she asked.

One last day. And one last night.

There was a pain inside her that she should not be feeling. Must not let herself feel.

But she felt it all the same.

Marc executed a fast, hard tack and brought the yacht about. His eyes went to Tara, ducking under the boom and then straightening. Her windblown hair was a halo around her face as she pushed it back with long fingers, refastening the loosened tendrils into a knot.

How beautiful she looked! Her face was alight, her

fabulous body gracefully leaning back, and her eyes were the colour of the green-blue sea.

One thought and one thought alone burned in his head. *I don't want this time with her to end.*

How could he? How could he want it to end when it had been so good? All the promise that she had held for him, all that instant powerful allure she'd held for him from the very first moment he'd set eyes on her, had been fulfilled.

He knew, with the rational part of him, that had he never had to resort to employing her to keep Hans's wife at bay he would never have chosen to follow through on that initial rush of desire. He'd have quenched it, turned aside from it, walked away. Hell, he wouldn't even have known she existed, would he? He'd never have gone to that fashion show had it not been for Celine…

But he had gone, he had seen her, and he had used her to thwart Hans's wife…

He had brought her into his life.

Had rewarded himself with her.

His grip on the tiller tightened. *It's been good. Better than good. Like nothing else in my life has ever been.*

From the first he'd known he wanted her—but these days together had been so much more than he'd thought they could be! He watched as she leant back, elbows on the gunwale, lifting her face to the sun, eyes closed, face in repose as they skimmed over the water, her hair billowing in the wind, surrounding her face again.

He felt something move within him.

I don't want this to end.

Those words came again—stronger now. And bringing more with them.

So don't end it. Take her with you to New York.

His thoughts flickered. Why shouldn't he? She could be with him in New York as easily as she was here. It could be just as good as it was here.

So take her with you.

The thought stayed in his head, haunting him, for the rest of the day. As he moored the yacht at the villa's jetty, phoned for it to be taken back to harbour. As they washed off the salt spray in the pool, then showered and dressed for dinner. As they met on the terrace for their customary cocktails.

It was with him all the time, hovering like a background thought, always present. Always tempting.

It was there all through dinner—ordered by him to be the absolute best his chef could conjure up—and all through the night they spent together…the long, long night in each other's arms. It was there as he brought her time and time again to the ecstasy that burned within her like a living flame, and it seemed to him that it burned more fiercely than it ever had, that his own possession of her was more urgent than it ever had been, their passion more searing than he could bear…

Yet afterwards, as she lay trembling in his arms, as he soothed her, stroked her dampened hair, held her silk-soft body to his, his unseeing gaze was troubled. And later still, when in the chill before the dawn he rose from their bed, winding a towel around his hips and walking out onto the balcony, closing his hands over the cold metal rail, and looking out over the dark sea beyond, his thoughts were uncertain.

If he took her with him to New York, what then? Would he take her back to France? To Paris? To stay with him at his hotel? Make her part of his life? His normal, working life?

And then what? What more would he want? And what more would *she* want…?

Again that same disturbing thought came to him— that she, too, might be remembering his impulsive declaration that afternoon, casting her as his intended wife, his fiancée, the future Madame Derenz.

Foreboding filled him. Unease. He did not know what she might want—could not know. All he knew was how he lived his life—and why. Just to have this time with her he'd already broken all the rules he lived by—rules that he'd had every reason to keep and none to break.

It had been good, this time he'd had with Tara— oh, so much more than good! But would it stay good? Or would danger start to lap at him…? Destroying what had been good?

Was it better simply to have this time—the memory of this time—and be content with that? Lest he live to regret a choice he should not have made…? Their time here had been idyllic—but could idylls last? *Should* they last?

He moved restlessly, unquiet in his mind.

He heard a sound behind him—bare feet—and

turned. She was naked, her wanton hair half covering her breasts, half revealing them.

'Come back to bed,' she said, her voice low, full with desire.

She held out a hand to him—a hand he took—and he went with her.

To possess her one last time…

Their bodies lay entwined, enmeshed. He stroked back the tumbled mass of her hair, eased his body from hers. Tara reached out her hand, her fingertips grazing the contours of his face. The ecstasy he'd given her was ebbing, and in its place another emotion was flowing.

She felt her heart squeeze and longing fill her. A silent cry breaking from her. *Don't let this be the last time! Oh, let it not be the last time for ever!*

A longing not to lose him, to lose *this*, flooded through her. Her eyes searched his in the dim light. When she spoke her throat was tight, her words hesitant, infused with longing. 'I could come to New York with you…' she said.

The hand stroking her hair stilled. In the dim light she saw his expression change. Close. Felt a coldness go through her.

'That wouldn't work,' he answered her.

She heard the change in his voice. The note of withdrawal. She dropped her eyes, unable to bear seeing him now. Seeing his face close against her, shutting her out.

She took a narrowed breath and closed her eyes,

saying no more. And as he drew her back against him, cradling her body, and she felt his breath warm on her bare shoulder, he knew that what they'd had, they had no longer. And never could again.

Behind her, with her long, slender back drawn against his chest, his arm thrown around her hips, Marc looked out over the darkened room. He had answered as he'd had to. With the only safe answer to give her. The answer that he had known must be his only answer from the very first.

CHAPTER NINE

TARA WOKE, STIRRING slowly to a consciousness she did not want. And as she roused herself from sleep and the world took shape around her she knew that it was already too late.

Marc was gone.

Cold filled her, like iced water flooding through her veins. A cry almost broke from her, but she suppressed it. What use to cry out? What use to cry at all?

This had always been going to happen—always!

But it was one thing to know that and another to feel it. To feel the empty place where he had been. To know that he would never come back to her. Never hold her in his arms again…

She felt her throat constrict, her face convulse. Slowly, with limbs like lead, she sat up, pushing her tangled hair from her face, shivering slightly, though the mid-morning sunlight poured into the room.

She looked around her blankly, as if Marc might suddenly materialise. But he never would again—and she knew that from the heaviness that was weighing her down. Knew it in the echo of his voice, telling her he did not want to take her with him. Knew it with even greater certainty as her eyes went to an envelope propped against the bedside lamp...and worse—oh, far worse—to the slim box propping it up.

She read the card first, the words blurring, then coming into focus.

You were asleep so I did not wake you. All is arranged for your flight to London. I wish you well—our time together has been good.

It was simply signed *Marc*. Nothing more.

Nothing except the cheque for ten thousand pounds at which she could only stare blankly, before replacing numbly into the envelope with the brief note.

Nothing except the ribbon of glittering emeralds in the jewellery case, catching the sunlight in a dazzle of gems. She let it slide through her fingers, knowing she should replace it in its velvet bed, leave it there on the bedside table. It was a gift far too valuable to accept. Impossible to accept.

But it was also impossible not to clutch it to her breast, to feel the precious gems indent her skin. To treasure it all her life.

How can I spurn his only gift to me? It's all that I will have to remember him by.

For a while she sat alone in the wide bed, as if making her farewells to it and all that had been there for her, with him. Then, at length, she knew she must move—must get up, must go back to her own bedroom, shower and dress, pack and leave. Go back to her own life. To her own reality.

The reality that did not have Marc in it. That *could* not have him in it.

I knew this moment would come. And now it has.

But what she had not known was how unbearable it would be… She had not been prepared for that. For the tearing ache in her throat. For the sense of loss. Of parting for ever.

It wasn't supposed to be like this! To feel like this!

The cry came from deep within her. From a place that should not exist, but did.

No, it was *not* supposed to be like this. It was supposed to have been nothing more than an indulgence of the senses…a yielding to her overpowering attraction to him…a time to be enjoyed, relished and revelled in, no more than that.

She should be leaving now, heading back to her own life, with a smile of fond remembrance on her face, with a friendly farewell and a little glow inside her after having had such a wonderful break from her reality!

That was what she was supposed to be feeling now. Not this crushing weight on her lungs…this constricted throat that choked her breath…this desperate sense of loss…

With a heavy heart she slipped through the connecting door. She had to go—leave. However hard, it had to be done.

Two maids were already in her room, carefully

packing the expensive clothes Marc had provided for her—an eternity ago, it seemed to her. She frowned at the sight. She must not take them with her. They were couture numbers, worth a fortune, and they were not hers to take.

She said as much to the maids, who looked confused.

'Monsieur Derenz has instructed for them to go with you, *mademoiselle*,' one said.

Tara shook her head. She had the emerald necklace—that was the only memory of Marc she would take, and only because it was his gift to her. That was its value—nothing else.

On sudden impulse, she said to the two young girls, '*You* have the clothes! Share them between you! They can be altered to fit you… Or maybe you could sell them?'

Their faces lit up disbelievingly, and Tara knew she could not take back her words. She was glad to have said them.

It was the only gladness she felt that day. What else had she to be glad about? That tearing feeling seemed to be clawing at her, ripping her apart, her throat was still choked, and that heaviness in her lungs, in her limbs weighing her down, was still there as she sat back in the chauffeured car, as she was whisked to the airport, as she boarded her flight.

He had booked her first-class.

The realisation made her throat clutch, telling her how much things had changed since her arrival.

My whole life has changed—because of Marc…

It was not until a fortnight later, as she checked her calendar with sudden, hollowing realisation, that she knew just how much…

Marc stood on the terrace of his penthouse residence in one of Manhattan's most luxurious hotels, staring out over the glittering city. His meeting was over, and the client was pleased and satisfied with what Bank Derenz had achieved for him. Now, with the evening ahead of him, Marc shifted restlessly.

There was something else he wanted.

Someone.

I want Tara—I want her here with me now. To enjoy the evening with me. I want to take her to dinner, to see her smile lighting up her eyes—sometimes dazzling, sometimes teasing, sometimes warm with laughter. I want to talk about whatever it was we used to talk about, in that conversation that seemed to flow so freely and naturally. And, yes, sometimes I want to spar with her, to hear her sometimes deadpan irony and those sardonic quips that draw a smile from me even now as I remember them…

And after dinner we'd come back here, and she'd be standing beside me, my arm around her, all of Manhattan glittering just for us. And she'd lift her face to mine, her eyes aglow, and I would catch her lips with mine and sweep her up, take her to my bed…

He could feel his body ache with desire for her, the blood heating in his veins.

With an effort of sheer will he tore his mind away from that beguiling scene so vivid in his head. He must not dwell on the woman he had left sleeping that morning, her oh-so-beautiful body naked in his bed, her glorious hair swathed across the pillow, her high, rounded breasts rising and falling with the gentle sound of her breathing.

It had been hard to leave her. Hard to reject her plea to come with him. Harder than he'd wanted it to be. Harder than it should have been. Harder than it was safe to have been—

But the safe thing for him to do had been to leave her. He knew that—knew it for all the reasons that had made him so wary of yielding as he had…yielding to his desire for her.

And the fact that he wanted to yield to it again, that his body so longed to do so, that he wanted to phone her now, tell her a flight was booked for her and that she should join him in New York, must make him even more wary.

It isn't safe to want her. It isn't safe because it's what she wants too. She asked outright—asked to come with me, wanted more than what we had in France. How much more would she have asked of me? Expected of me?

That was the truth of it. The harsh, necessary truth he'd always had to live his life by.

His eyes shadowed, thoughts turbid. He was making himself face what he did not want to face, but must—as he always had.

If I bring her here…keep her with me…how can I know if it's me she's choosing or Banc Derenz?

That was the reason he now turned away from the plate-glass window overlooking the city far below.

His thoughts went back to when he had last set eyes on her, sleeping so peacefully in his bed. He had slipped past her, to the bedside table, where he had placed the farewell note he had scrawled. And his gift for her.

The gift that would part him from her for ever. The gift that he'd left, quite deliberately, to tell her that what they'd had was over.

To tell *himself*…

Tara leant against the window frame of her bedroom at the cottage, breathing in the night air of the countryside. So sweet and fresh after the polluted traffic fumes of London. An owl hooted in the distance, and that was the only sound.

No ceaseless murmurings of cicadas, no sound of the sea lapping at the rocky shore, no scent of flowers too delicate for England…

No Marc beside her, gazing out over the wine-dark sea with her, listening to the soft Mediterranean night, his arm warm around her, drawing her against his body, before he turned her to him, lowered his mouth to hers, led her indoors to his bed, to his embrace…

She felt her heart twist, her body fill with longing.

But to what purpose?

Marc was gone from her life and she from his. She must accept it—accept what had happened and accept everything about the life she faced now.

Accept that what I feel for him, for the loss of him,

is not what I thought I would feel. Accept that there is nothing I can do about it but what I am doing now. Accept that what I'm doing is all that I can do. All that can happen now.

Her expression changed as she gazed out over the shadowy garden edged by trees and the fields beyond.

How utterly her life had changed! How totally. All because of Marc…

She felt emotion crush within her. Should she regret what she had done? Wish that it had not happened? That it had not changed her so absolutely?

How *could* she regret it?

She gave a sigh—but not one of happiness. Nor of unhappiness. It was an exquisitely painful mix of both.

I can think of neither—feel neither. Not together.

Separately, yes, each one could fill her being. They were contradictory to one another. But they never cancelled each other out. Only…bewildered her. Tormented her.

She felt emotion buckling her. Oh, to have such joy and such pain combined!

She felt her hand clutch what she was holding, then made herself open her palm, gaze down at what was within. In the darkness the vivid colour of the precious gems was not visible, yet it still seemed to glow with a light of its own.

It was a complication she must shed.

I should never have taken it! Never kept it to remember him by!

She felt the emotion that was so unbearable, buckle

her again. For one long moment she continued to gaze at what she held. Then slowly, very slowly, she closed her hand again.

She had kept it long enough—far too long. It must be returned. She must not keep it. Could not. Not now. *Especially not now.*

The emotion came again, convulsing her, stronger than ever. Oh, sense and rational thought and every other worldly consideration might cry out against what she was set on—but they could not prevail. *Must* not.

I know what I must do and I will do it.

With a slow, heavy movement she withdrew from the window, crossed over to the little old-fashioned dressing table that had once been her grandmother's and let fall what she held in her hand.

The noise of its fall was muffled by the piece of paper onto which it slithered. That, too, must be returned. And when it had been the last link with Marc would be severed. *Almost* the last...

She turned away, her empty hand slipping across her body. There was one thing that would always bind them, however much he no longer wanted her. But she must never tell him. For one overwhelming reason.

Because he does not want me. He is done with me. He has made that crystal-clear. His rejection of me is absolute.

So it did not matter, did it? Anything else could not matter.

However good it was, it was only ever meant to be for that brief time. I knew that, and so did he, and that is what we both intended. That is what I must hold in my head now. And what he gave me to show me that he had done with me, so that I understood and accepted it, must go back to him. Because it is the right and the only thing to do.

And when it was gone she would get on with the life that awaited her now. With all its pain and joy. Joy and pain. Mingling for ever now.

Marc was back in Paris. After New York he'd had the sudden urge to catch up with all his affairs in the Americas, making an extensive tour of branches of Banc Derenz from Quebec to Buenos Aires, which had taken several weeks. There had been no pressing need—at least not from a business perspective—but it had seemed a good idea to him, all the same, for reasons he'd had no wish to examine further.

The tour had served its purpose—putting space and time between those heady, carefree days at the villa and the rest of his life.

Now, once more in Paris, he was burying himself in work and an endless round of socialising in which he had no interest at all, but knew it was necessary.

And yet neither the tour of the Americas, nor his current punishing workload, nor the endless round of social engagements he was busying himself with were having the slightest effect.

He still wanted Tara. Wanted her back in his life. The one woman he wanted but should not want.

With the same restlessness that had dominated him since he'd flown to New York a few months ago he looked out over the Parisian cityscape, wanting Tara there with him.

He glanced at his watch without enthusiasm. His car would be waiting for him, ready to take him to the Paris Opera, where he was entertaining two of his clients and their daughter. His mouth tightened. The daughter was making it clear that she would be more than happy for him to pay her attention for reasons other than the fact that her parents banked at Banc Derenz. And she was not alone in her designs and hopes.

He gave an angry sigh. The whole damn circus was starting up again. Women in whom he had no interest at all, seeking his attention.

Women who were not Tara.

He shut his eyes. *I'll get over her. In time I'll forget her. I have to.*

He knew it must happen one day, but it was proving harder than he had thought it would. *Damnably* harder.

It was showing too, and he was grimly aware of that. Aware that, just as he'd been when Celine had plagued him, he was more short-tempered, having little patience either for demanding clients or fellow directors.

A bear with a sore head.

That was the expression he'd used to Tara.

Who was no longer in his life. And could never be again. However much he wanted her. *Because* he wanted her.

That was the danger, he knew. The danger that

his desire for her would make him weak…make him ready to believe—want to believe—that his wealth was not the reason at all for her to be with him.

He'd believed that once before in his life—and it had been the biggest mistake he'd ever made. Thinking he was important to Marianne. When all along it had only been the Derenz money.

And the fact that Tara valued the Derenz money was evident. Right from the start she'd been keen on it—from that paltry five hundred pounds for chaperoning Celine back to her hotel to the ten thousand pounds she'd demanded for going to France.

And she had taken those emeralds he'd left for her. Helped herself to them as her due—just as readily as she'd helped herself to the couture wardrobe he'd supplied.

Oh, she might not be a gold-digger—nothing so repellent—but it was undeniable that she had enjoyed the luxury of his lifestyle, the valuable gifts he'd given her. And that was a danger sign—surely it was?

If I take her back she'll get used to that luxury lifestyle…start taking it for granted. Not wanting to lose it. It will become important to her. More important to her than I am. And soon would it be me she wanted—or just the lifestyle I could provide for her?

He felt that old, familiar wariness filling him. Restlessly, he shifted again, tugging at the cuffs of his tuxedo.

What point was there in going over and over the reasons he must resist the urge to get back in touch with her, to resume what they had had, seek to extend it? However powerful that urge, he had to resist it. He must. Anything else was just too risky.

The doors of the elegant salon were opening and a staff member stood there, presumably to inform Marc that his car was awaiting him. But the man had a silver salver in his hand, upon which Marc could see an envelope.

With a murmur of thanks he took it, then stilled. Staring down at it. It had a UK stamp. And it was handwritten in a hand he had come to recognise.

He felt a clenching of his stomach, a tightening of his muscles. A sudden rush of blood.

What had Tara written? *Why?*

His face expressionless, belying a melee of thoughts behind its impassive mask, he opened it. Unfolded the single sheet of paper within and forced his eyes to read the contents.

The words leapt at him.

Marc,
I am not going to cash your cheque. What started out as a job did not end that way, and it would be very wrong of me to expect you to be bound by that original agreement.

Also, but for different reasons, I cannot keep the beautiful necklace you left for me. I am sure you only meant to be generous, but you must see how impossible it is for me to accept so very expensive a gift. Please do not be offended by this. I shall have it couriered back to you.

By the same token, nor can I accept the gift

*of all the couture clothes you provided for me.
I hope you do not mind, but I gave them to the
maids—they were so thrilled. Please do not be
angry with them for accepting.*

*I'm sorry this has taken me so long, but I've
been very busy working. My life is about to
take me in a quite different direction and I shall
be leaving London, and modelling, far behind.*

It was simply signed with her name. Nothing more.

The words on the page seemed to blur and shift
and come again into focus. Slowly, very slowly, the
hand holding the letter dropped to his side.

His heart seemed to be thumping in his chest as
if he'd just done a strenuous workout. As if a crushing weight had been lifted off him. An impenetrable
barrier just…dissolved. Gone.

He stared out across the room. The member of staff
was standing in the doorway again.

'Your car is ready, Monsieur Derenz,' he intoned.

Marc frowned. He wasn't going to the opera. Not
tonight. It was out of the question. A quite different
destination beckoned.

The thud of his heartbeat was getting stronger.
Deafening him. The letter in his hand seemed to be
burning his fingers. He looked across at the man,
nodded at him. Gave him his instructions. New instructions.

An overnight bag to prepare, a car to take him to
Le Bourget, not the Paris Opéra. Regrets to be sent
to his guests. And a flight to London to organise.

As the man departed only one word burned in Marc's head, seared in his body. *Tara!*

She had taken nothing from him—absolutely nothing. Not the money she'd earned, nor the couture wardrobe, nor the emerald necklace. Nothing at all! So what did that say about her?

Emotion held in check for so many punishing weeks, so many self-denying days and nights, exploded within him. Distilled into one single realisation. One overpowering impulse.

I can have her back.

Tara, the woman he wanted—*still* wanted!—and now he could have her again.

Nothing he had ever felt before had felt so good…

CHAPTER TEN

TARA WAS WALKING along the hard London pavements as briskly as she could in the heat. Summer had arrived with a vengeance, and the city was sticky and airless after the fresh country air. She was tired, and the changes in her body were starting to make themselves felt.

She'd travelled up from Dorset by train that morning and gone straight to her appointments. The first had been with a modelling agency specialising in the only shoots she'd be able to do soon, to see if they would take her on when that became necessary. The other, which she'd just come from, had been with her bank, to go through her finances.

Now that she could no longer count on the ten thousand pounds from Marc, it was going to be hard to move to Dorset immediately. Yet doing so was imperative—she had to settle into her new life as quickly as she could, while she was still unencumbered. She would need to buy a car, for a start—a second-hand one—for she would not be able to manage without one, and she still hadn't renovated the kitchen and the bathroom as planned.

She'd hoped that her bank might let her raise a small mortgage to tide her over, but the answer had not been encouraging—her future income to service the debt was going to be uncertain, to say the least. She was not a good risk.

It would have been so much easier if I could have kept that ten thousand pounds...

The thought hovered in her head and she had to dismiss it sharply. Yes, keeping it would have been the prudent thing to do—even if Marc would never know why—but as he *could* never know, she could not possibly keep it.

It was the same stricture that applied to her destination now, and her reason for going there. Yes, the prudent thing to do now would be to sell the necklace, realise its financial value, and bank that for all that she would need in the years ahead. But she had resisted that temptation, knowing what she must do. It was impossible for her to keep his parting gift!

Her letter to him, which he must have received now, for she had posted it from Dorset several days ago, had made that clear. Perhaps he was accustomed to gifting expensive jewellery to the women he had affairs with—but to such women, coming as they did from his über-rich world, something like that emerald necklace would be a mere bagatelle! To her, however, it was utterly beyond her horizon.

If he had only given me a token gift—of little monetary value. I could have kept that willingly, oh, so willingly, as a keepsake!

Her expression changed. More than a keepsake. A legacy…

She shied her mind away. She could see her destination—only a little way away now. The exclusive Mayfair jeweller she was going to ask to courier the necklace back to Marc. They would know how to do it—how to ensure the valuable item reached him securely, as she had written to him that it would.

Once it was gone she would feel easier in her mind. The temptation to keep it, against all her conscience, would be gone from her, no longer to be wrestled with. Her eyes shadowed, as they did so often now. And she need no longer wrestle with a temptation so much greater than merely keeping the emeralds.

She heard it echo now in her head—what had called to her so longingly… *Tell him—just tell him!*

Oh, how she wanted to! So much!

But she knew she was clutching at dreams—dreams she must not have. Dreams Marc had made *clear* she must not have.

Wearily, she put her thoughts aside. She had been through them, gone round and round, and there was no other conclusion to be drawn. Marc had finished with her and she must not hope for anything else.

Not even now.

Especially not now.

Deliberately she quickened her pace, walking up to the wide, imposing doors. A security guard stood there, very visibly, and as she approached moved to open the electronically controlled doors for her. But just as they opened, someone walked out.

'Fraulein Tara! *Was fur eine Uberraschung!*'

She halted, totally taken aback. Hans Neuberger came up to her, pleasure on his kindly face, as well as the surprise he'd just exclaimed over seeing her.

'How very good to see you again!' he said in his punctilious manner. 'And how glad I am to do so.' He smiled. 'This unexpected but delightful encounter provides me with an excellent opportunity! I wonder,' he went on, his voice politely enquiring, 'whether you would care to join me for lunch? I hope that you will say yes. Unless, of course,' he added, 'you have another engagement perhaps?'

'Um—no. I mean, that is…' Tara floundered, not really knowing what to say. She was trying to get her head around seeing Hans again, since the last time she'd seen him had been just after that party on the yacht in Cannes, with Celine's dreadful friends…

'Oh, then, please, it would be so very kind of you to indulge me in this request.'

His kindly face was smiling and expectant. It would be hard to say no, and she did not wish to hurt his feelings, however tumultuous hers were at seeing him again, which had plunged her head back to the time she'd spent in France. So, numbly, she let him guide her across the street where she saw, with a little frisson of recognition, the side entrance to a hotel that stung in her memory.

This was the hotel where Marc had deposited Celine that first fateful evening…

Emotion wove through her, but Hans was ushering her inside. His mood seemed buoyant, and he was far less crushed than he'd been at Marc's villa. Getting Celine out of his life clearly suited him.

And so he informed her—though far more generously than Celine deserved. 'I was not able to make her happy,' he said sadly as they took their places in the hotel restaurant. 'So it is good, I think, that she has now met another man who can. A Russian, this time! They are currently sailing the Black Sea on his new yacht. I am glad for her…'

Tactfully, Tara forbore to express her views on how the self-serving Celine had latched on to yet another rich man. Hans's face had brightened, and he was changing the subject.

'But that is quite enough about myself! Tell me, if you please, a little of what is happening with *you*?' His expression changed. 'I have, alas, been preoccupied with—well, all the business of setting Celine free, as she wishes to be. But I very much hope all is still well with you and Marc.'

There was only polite enquiry in his question, yet Tara froze. Floundering, she struggled for something to say. Anything…

'No—that is to say Marc and I— Well, we are no longer together.'

She saw Hans's face fall. 'I am sorry to hear that,' he said. His eyes rested on her and there was more than his habitual kindness in them. 'You were, I think, very good for Marc.' He paused, as if finding the right words. 'He is possessed of a character that can be very…*forceful*, perhaps is the way to describe him. You were—how can I express this?—a good match for him.'

'Yes,' Tara said ruefully. 'I did stand up to him—it's not my nature to back down.'

Hans gave a little laugh. 'Two equal forces meeting,' he said.

She looked at him. 'Yes, and then parting. As we have. Whatever there was,' she said firmly, 'is now finished.'

Hans's eyes were on her still, and she wished they weren't.

'That is a pity,' he said. 'I wish it were otherwise,'

She took a breath. 'Yes, well, there it is. Marc and I had a…a lovely time together… But, well, it ran its course and that is that.'

She wanted to change the subject—any way she could. Her throat had tightened, and she didn't want it to. Seeing Hans again had brought everything back in vivid memory. And she didn't want that. Couldn't bear it. It just hurt too much.

'So,' she said, with determined brightness as the waiters brought over the menus, 'what brings you to London? Have you been here long?'

Thankfully, Hans took her lead. 'I arrived only this morning,' he said. 'My son Bernhardt will be joining me this evening with his fiancée. They are making a little holiday here. His mother-in-law-to-be is accompanying them. She was a close friend of my wife—my *late* wife—and, like me, was most sadly widowed a few years ago. We have always got on very well, both sharing the loss of our spouses, and now, with the engagement of our children, we have much in common. So much so that—well,' he went on in a little rush of open emotion, 'once my divorce from Celine is finalised, Ilse and I plan to make our future together. Our children could not be more delighted!'

A smile warmed Tara's expression. 'Oh, that's wonderful!' she exclaimed.

Just as she'd hoped, the kindly Hans would be marrying again—happily this time, surely? Such a match sounded ideal.

He leant forward. 'You may have wondered,' he said, 'why I was emerging from that so very elegant jeweller's when I encountered you—'

Tara hadn't wondered—had been too taken aback to do anything of the sort—but she didn't say so. Anyway, Hans was busy slipping a hand inside his jacket, removing from it a small cube of a box. Tara did not need X-ray vision to know what it would contain.

He held it towards her, opening it. 'Do you think she will like this?' he asked.

There was such warmth, such hope in his voice, that Tara could not help but let a smile of equal warmth light up her own face.

'It's *beautiful*!' she exclaimed, unable to resist touching the exquisite diamond engagement ring within. 'She will *adore* it!' Spontaneously, she reached her hand to his sleeve. 'She's a lucky, *lucky* woman!' she told him.

And then, because she was glad for him—glad for anyone who had found a happiness that for herself could never be—her expression softened.

'Let me be the very first to congratulate you,' she said. And she kissed him on the cheek, an expression of open delight on her face.

Marc sat in his chauffeured car, frustration etched into his expression. He was burning to find Tara—the imperative was driving him like an unstoppable tide, flooding over him.

He was free. Free to take her back. Free to claim her, to make her his again. There was nothing to stop him, to block him—not any more. Had she been anything like he'd feared she would never have written that letter to him—never have said what she had.

He took it out of his jacket pocket again now, read it again, as he had read it over and over, his eyes alight.

Their expression changed back to frustration. To know that he was free to take her back, to renew what had been between them and yet not to be able to find her…! It was intolerable—unbearable.

But she was not to be found.

He had gone to her flat last night, heading there the moment the private jet from Le Bourget had landed at City Airport, after urging the car through the traffic, to be told in an offhand fashion by a flatmate that she was away, and they had no idea where.

Thwarted, he had had to repair to his hotel, to kick his heels, and thence to interrogate her modelling agency first thing that morning—only to be informed that she had no modelling engagements that day and that they had no idea where she was and did not care. For reasons of confidentiality they would not give him her mobile number—which he, for reasons now utterly incomprehensible to him, had never known. They would let him know he was trying to contact her, and that was all.

He glowered, face dark, eyes flashing with frustration, as the car moved off into the London traffic. He had occupied himself by calling in on the branch of Banc Derenz in Mayfair, but now he was hungry.

He did not want the manager's company for lunch. He didn't want anyone's company. *Only one person.*

It burned within him…his sense of urgency, his mounting sense of frustration that he had come to London to find her—claim her. To throw lifelong caution to the winds and to ride the instinct that was driving him now, that her letter had let loose, like a tidal wave carrying him forward…

His car pulled up at his hotel. The very same hotel where he'd deposited Celine the first night that Tara had come into his life.

He'd wanted her then—had felt that kick of desire from the first moment of seeing her, so unwillingly responding to his impatient summons at that benighted fashion show, had felt it kick again when she'd sat beside him in the limo, and yet again creaming in his veins as, with a deliberate gesture, he'd taken her hand to kiss her wrist…to show her that she might be as hostile, as back-talking as she liked, but she was not immune to him, to what was flaring like marsh fire between them…

A smile played at his mouth, as his mind revolved those memories and so many more since then...

And all those yet to come.

Immediately his imagination leapt to the challenge. Their first night together again... The sensual bliss would burn between them as it always had, every time!

His mind ran on, leaping from image to image. And afterwards a holiday—only the two of them. Wherever she wanted to go. The Caribbean, or maybe the Maldives, the Seychelles? The South Seas? Wherever in the world she wanted. Wherever they could have a tropical island entirely to themselves...

Nights under the stars...days on silver beaches... disporting ourselves in turquoise lagoons...lazing beneath palm fronds waving gently in the tropical breeze...

Anticipation filled him, surging in his blood...

The chauffeur was opening his door and he vaulted out. He would grab lunch, and then interrogate that damn agency of hers again. He'd already sent one of his staff from the London branch of Derenz to doorstep her flat, lest she arrive there unexpectedly.

She's here somewhere. I just have to find her.

Find her and get her back. Back into his life— where she belonged.

He strode into the hotel, fuelled with the urgency now driving him...consuming him. Filled with elation—with an impatience to find her again that was burning in his veins. To have her unforgettable beauty before him once again...

'Mr Derenz, good afternoon. Will you be lunching with us today?'

The polite enquiry at the entrance to the restaurant interrupted his vision.

'Yes,' he said distractedly, impatiently.

His glance needled around the restaurant.

And froze.

The image in his head—the one his eyes had frozen on—solidified.

Tara—it was *Tara*. Here. Right in front of him. Across the dining room. Sitting at one of the tables.

There was someone with her—someone with his back to him.

Someone that Tara was looking at. Gazing at.

Smiling at, her face alight with pleasure and delight.

He saw the man she was smiling at offer something to her, saw the flash as it caught the sunlight. Saw her lean forward a little, reach out a long, slender forearm. Saw what it was that she touched with her index finger, how the delight in her eyes lit her whole face.

Saw her lean closer now, across the table, saw her bestow a kiss upon the cheek of the man he now recognised.

Saw blackness fill his vision. Blinding him...

Memory seared into his blinded sight.

Marianne across that restaurant, sitting with another man, his diamond glittering on her finger, holding up her hand for Marc to see...

Still blinded, he lurched away.

There was blackness in his soul...

* * *

Just as she brushed her soft kiss of congratulation on Hans's lined cheek, Tara's gaze slipped past him.

And widened disbelievingly.

Marc?

For a second emotion leapt in her, soaring upwards. Then a fraction of a section later it crashed.

In that minute space of time she had registered two things. That he had seen her. And that he had turned on his heel and was walking out of the restaurant again as rapidly as the mesh of tables would allow him.

That told her one thing, and one thing only. He had not wanted to see her. Or acknowledge her presence there.

She felt a vice crushing her as she sat back in her seat, unable to breathe. She urgently had to regain control of herself. If Hans noticed her reaction he might wonder why. If he turned he might see Marc leaving the restaurant. Might go after him…drag him back to their table. She would have to encounter Marc again—Marc who had turned and bolted rather than speak to her.

If she'd ever wanted proof that he was over her—that he wanted *nothing* more to do with her—she had it now. Brutally and incontrovertibly!

The vice around her lungs squeezed more tightly. *I've got to get out of here!*

She didn't dare risk it! Didn't dare risk an encounter with him that he so obviously did not want! It would be mortifying.

'Hans, I'm so sorry, but I'm afraid I don't have time for lunch after all.' The excuse sounded impolite, but she had to give it. 'Do please forgive me!'

She got to her feet; Hans promptly did the same.

'I'm so very pleased for you—you and Ilse.' She tried to infuse warmth into her voice but she was keeping an eye on the exit to the hotel lobby. Was it clear of Marc yet? If she could just get to the corridor leading to the side entrance Hans had brought her in by she could escape...

She got away from Hans. He looked slightly bewildered by her sudden departure, but it could not be helped. At the door to the restaurant she glanced towards the revolving doors at the main entrance, leading to the street, then whirled around to head towards the side entrance.

Just as a tall, immovable figure turned abruptly away from the reception desk, out of her eyeline.

She cannoned into it.

It was Marc.

CHAPTER ELEVEN

SHE GAVE AN audible cry—she couldn't stop it—and lurched backwards as quickly as she could. He automatically reached up his hands to steady her, then dropped them, as if he might scald himself on her.

She couldn't think straight—couldn't do anything at all except stumble another step backwards and blurt out, 'Marc—I... I thought you had left the hotel.'

Marc's face hardened. The livid emotion that had flashed through him as she'd bumped into him turning away from the reception desk was being hammered down inside him. He would not let it show. *Would not.* He'd been cancelling his reservation for that night. What point and what purpose to stay now? he thought savagely.

He knew he had to say something, but how could he? The only words he wanted to hurl at her were... pointless. So all he said, his voice as hard and as expressionless as his face was, 'I am just leaving.'

Had she come running after him?

But why should she? She has no need of me now!

The words seared across his naked synapses as

if they were red-hot. No, Tara had no need of him now—no need at all!

Savage fury bit like a wolf.

Hans! God in heaven—Hans, of all men! Beaming like a lovesick idiot, offering her that ring...that glittering, iridescent diamond ring! For her to reach for. To take for herself. Just as Marianne had.

Fury bit again, but its savagery was not just rage. It was worse than rage. Oh, *so* much worse...

Yet he would not let her see it. That, at least, he would deny her!

She was looking up at him, consternation in her face. Was she going to try and explain herself—justify herself? It sickened him even to think about it.

But she made no reference to the scene he knew she had seen him witness. Instead she seemed to be intent on attempting some kind of mockery of a conversation.

'So am I,' he heard her say. 'Just leaving the hotel.'

Tara heard her own words and paled. *Oh, God, don't let him think I'm angling for a lift! Please, please, no!*

Memory, hot and humiliating, came to her, of how she had asked to go to New York with him—and the unhesitating rejection she had received. She felt that same mortification burning in her again, that he might think she had come racing after him.

This whole encounter was a nightmare, an ordeal so excruciating she couldn't bear it. He was radiating on every frequency the fact that seeing her again was the last thing he wanted. His stance was stiff and tense, his expression closed and forbidding. He could not have made it plainer to her that he did not want to talk to her. Did not want to have anything at all to do with her any more.

He wants nothing to do with me! He didn't even want to come over and say hello—not even to his friend Hans!

Could anything have rammed home to her just how much Marc Derenz did *not* want her any longer? That all he wanted was to be shot of her?

Her chin came up—it cost her all her strength, but she did it. 'I must be on my way,' she said. She made her voice bright, but it was like squeezing it through a wringer inset with vicious spikes.

She paused. Swallowed. Thoughts and emotions tumbled violently within her, a feeling akin to panic. There was something she had to say to him. To make things clear to him. As crystal-clear as he was making them to her. That she, too, had moved on with her life. That she would make no claim on him at all. Not even as a casual acquaintance…

She felt emotion choke her, but forced herself to say what she had to. Reassure him that she knew, and accepted, that she was nothing to him any longer.

She had said as much in her letter to him and now she would say it again, to make sure he knew.

'I'll be moving away from London very soon. I'm getting out of modelling completely. I can't wait!' She forced enthusiasm into her voice, though every word was torn from her.

His stony expression did not change.

'I'm sure you will enjoy your future life,' he replied.

He spoke with absolute indifference, and it was like a blow.

'Thank you—yes, I shall. I have every intention of doing so!' she returned.

Pride came to her rescue. Ragged shreds of it, which she clutched around her for the pathetic protection she could get from it.

'Hans is still in the restaurant.' She made herself smile, forcing it across her face as if she were posing for a camera—putting it on, faking it, clinging to it as if it were a life raft. 'I'm sure that he will want to see you! He has such exciting news! Best you hear it from him…'

She was speaking almost at random, in staccato ramblings. She could not bear to see his face, his indifferent expression, as he so clearly waited for her to leave him alone, to take himself off. She shifted her handbag from one hand to the other, and as she did so she jolted. Remembering something.

Something she might as well do here and now. To make an end to what had been between them and was now nothing more than him waiting impatiently for her to leave him be.

She raised her bag, snapping open the fastener.

'Marc—this is most opportune!' The words were still staccato. 'I was going to ask the jeweller across the road to courier this to you, as I promised, but you might as well take it yourself.'

She delved into her bag, extracted the jewellery case. Held it out to him expectantly.

His eyes lanced the box, then wordlessly he took it. His mouth seemed to tighten and she wondered why. Expressionlessly, he slid it into his inside jacket pocket.

For a second—just a second—she went on staring up at him. As if she would imprint his face on her memory with indelible ink.

Words formed in her head, etching like acid. *This is the last time I shall see him...*

The knowledge was drowning her, draining the blood from her.

'Goodbye, Marc,' she said. Her voice was faint.

She turned, plunging down the corridor. Eyes blind. Fleeing the man who did not want her any longer. Who would never want her again.

Whom she would never see again.

Anguish crushed her heart, and hot, burning tears started to roll silently down her cheeks. Such useless tears…

Marc stood, nailing a smile of greeting to his face as his guests arrived. It was the bank's autumn party, for its most valued clients, held at one of Paris's most famous hotels, and he had no choice but to host it. But there was one client whose presence here this evening he dreaded the most. Hans Neuberger.

Would he show up? He was one of the bank's most long-standing clients and had never missed this annual occasion. But now…?

Marc felt his mind slide sideways, not wanting to articulate his thoughts. All he knew was that he could not face seeing Hans again.

Will he bring her here?

That was the question that burned in him now, as he greeted his guests. What he said to them he didn't know. All that was in his head—all there had been all these weeks, since that unbearable day in London— was the scene he had witnessed. That nightmare scene that was blazoned inside his skull in livid, sickening neon.

Ineradicable—indelible.

Tara, leaning forward, her face alight. Hans offering that tell-tale box, its lid showing the exclusive logo of a world-famous jeweller, revealing the flash of the diamond ring within. And Tara reaching for it. Tara bestowing a kiss of gratitude on Hans's cheek with that glow in her face, her eyes…

Bitter acid flooded his veins. Just as it had all those years ago as he'd watched Marianne declare her faithlessness to the world. Declare to the world what she wanted. A rich, older man to pamper her…shower her with jewellery.

His face twisted. To think he had *rejoiced* that Tara had declined to cash the cheque he'd left for her! Had returned his emeralds.

Well, why wouldn't she? Now she has all Hans's wealth to squander on herself!

He stoked the savage anger within him. Thanks to *his* indulgence of her, she had got a taste for the high life! Had realised, when he'd left her, that she could not get that permanently from himself! So she'd targeted someone who could supply it permanently! Plying Hans with sympathy, with friendliness…

It was the very opposite of Celine's open scorn, but with the same end in mind. To get what she wanted—Hans's ring on her finger and his fortune hers to enjoy...

With a smothered oath he tore his mind away. What use to feel such fury? Such betrayal?

He had survived what Marianne had done to him. He would survive what Tara had inflicted upon him too.

Yet as the endless receiving line finally dwindled, with only a few late guests still arriving, he found his eyes going past the doors of the ornate function room to the head of the stairs leading up from the lobby.

Would she come here tonight with Hans?

He felt emotion churn within him.

But it was not anger. And with a sudden hollowing within him, he knew what the emotion was.

Longing.

He stilled. Closing his eyes momentarily. He knew that feeling. Knew its unbearable strength, its agony. Had felt it once before in his life.

After his parents had been killed.

The longing...the unbearable, agonising longing to see again those who were lost to him for ever.

As Tara was.

Tara who could never be his again...

'Marc—I am so sorry to arrive late!'

His eyes flashed open. It was Hans—alone.

He froze. Unable to say anything, anything at all. Unable to process any thoughts at all.

Hans was speaking again. 'We have been a little

delayed. Bernhardt is with me, and I hope you will not object but I have brought two other guests as well. Karin—Bernhardt's fiancée—and…' He smiled self-consciously as Marc stood, frozen. 'And one more.' And now Hans's smile broadened. 'One who has become very dear to me.'

Marc heard the words, saw Hans take a breath and then continue on, his eyes bright.

'Of course until my divorce is finalised no formal announcement can be made, and it has been necessary, therefore, to be discreet, so perhaps my news will be a surprise to you?'

Marc's expression darkened. 'No—I've known for weeks.' His voice was hard—as hard as tempered steel. His eyes flashed, vehemence filling his voice now, unable to stay silent. 'Hans, this is *madness*— to be caught again! Did you not learn enough from Celine? How can you possibly repeat the same disastrous mistake! For God's sake, man, however besotted you are, have the sense not to do this!'

He saw Hans's expression change from bewilderment to astonishment, and then to rejection. 'Marc,' he said stiffly, 'I am perfectly aware that Celine was, indeed, a very grave error of my judgement, but—'

'And so is *Tara*!' Marc's voice slashed across the other man's.

There was silence—complete silence. Around him Marc could hear the background chatter of voices, the clinking of glasses. And inside the thundering of his heartbeat, drowning out everything. Even his own voice.

'Did you think I hadn't seen you both, in London? You and Tara—' His voice twisted over her name. Choking on it. 'Did you think I didn't see the ring you were giving her? See how her face lit up? How she couldn't wait to take it from you? How eager she was to kiss you?'

Hans stared. Then spoke. *'Bist Du verukt?'*

Fury lashed across Marc's face. Insane? No, he was *not* insane! Filled with any number of violent emotions, but not that!

Then suddenly Hans's hand was closing over his sleeve with surprising force for a man his age. 'Marc—you could not *possibly* have thought—' He broke off, then spoke again. His tone brooked no contradiction. 'What you saw—whatever it is you *feared* you saw, Marc—was Tara's very kind reaction to the news I had just told her. Of my intention to remarry, yes, indeed. But if you think, for an instant, that *she* was the object of my intentions—'

Marc felt his arm released. Hans was turning aside, allowing three more people who had just entered the room to come up to them. Marc's eyes went to them. Bernhardt, a younger version of Hans, well-known to him, with a young, attractive woman on one arm. And on the other arm an older woman with similar looks to the younger one. A woman who was smiling at Hans with a fond, affectionate look on her face. And on the third finger of the hand tucked into Bernhardt's arm was a diamond ring…

Hans turned back to Marc and his tone was formal

now. 'You will permit me to introduce to you Frau Ilse Holz and her daughter Karin?'

His eyes rested on Marc.

'Ilse,' Marc heard him say, as if from a long way away, 'has done me the very great honour of agreeing, when the time is right, to make me the happiest of men. I know,' he added, 'that you will wish us well.'

Marc might have acknowledged the introduction. He might have said whatever was required of him. Might have been aware of Hans's gaze becoming speculative.

But of all of those things he had absolutely no awareness at all. Only one thought was in his head. One blinding thought. One absolute realisation. Burning in him.

And then Bernhardt was leading away his fiancée, and the woman who was to be both his mother-in-law and his stepmother, into the throng.

Hans paused. His eyes were not speculative now. They were filled with compassion. 'Go,' he said quietly, to Marc alone. 'This…here…' he gestured to the party all around them '…is not important. You have others to see to it. So—go, my friend.'

And Marc went. Needing no further telling…

CHAPTER TWELVE

A BLACKBIRD WAS hopping about on the lawn, picking at the birdseed which Tara had started to scatter each day now that autumn was arriving. A few late bees could be heard buzzing on what was left of the lavender. There was a mild, drowsy feel to the day, as if summer were disinclined to pack its bags completely and leave the garden, preferring to make a graceful handover to its successive season.

Tara was glad of it. Sitting out here in the still warm sunshine, wearing only a light sweater and cotton trousers, her feet in canvas shoes, was really very pleasant. The trees bordering the large garden backing on to the fields beyond were flushed with rich autumnal copper, but still shot through with summer's green. A time of transition, indeed.

It echoed her own mood. *A time of transition*. She might have finally made the move from London to Dorset some weeks ago, but it was only now that she was really feeling her move was permanent. As was so much else.

She flexed her body, already less ultra-slim than

she'd had to keep it during her modelling career. It was filling out, softening her features, rounding her abdomen, ripening her breasts.

Her mind seemed to be hovering, as the seasons were, between her old life and the one she was now embarked upon. She knew she must look ahead to the future—what else was there to do? She must embrace it—just as she must embrace the coming winter. Enjoy what it would offer her.

Her expression changed, her fingers tracing over her midriff absently. She must not regret the time that had gone and passed for ever—the brief, precious time she'd had during that summer idyll so long ago, so far away, beside that azure coast. No, she must never regret that time—even though she must accept that it was gone from her, never to return. That Marc was gone from her for ever.

A cry was stifled in her throat. Anguish bit deep within her.

I'll never see him again—never hear his voice again—never feel his mouth on mine, his hand in mine. Never see him smile, or laugh, or his eyes pool with desire... Never feel his body over mine, or hold him to me, or wind my arms around him...

Her eyes gazed out, wide and unseeing, over the autumnal garden. How had it happened that what she had entered into with Marc—something that had never been intended to be anything other than an indulgence of her overpowering physical response to him—had become what she now knew, with a clutching of her heart, to be what it would be for ever?

How had she come to fall in love with him?

She felt that silent cry in her throat again.

I fell in love with him and never knew it—not until he left me. Not until I knew I would never see him again. Never be part of his life...

Her hands spasmed over the arms of the padded garden chair and she felt that deep stab of anguish again.

But what point was there in feeling it? She had a future to make for herself—a future she *must* make. And not merely for her own sake. For the sake of the most precious gift Marc could have given her. Not the vast treasures of his wealth—that was dust and ashes to her! A gift so much more precious...

A gift he must never know he had given her...

Her grip on the arms of the chair slackened and she moved her hands across her body in a gesture as old as time...

She would never see Marc again, and the pain of that loss would never leave her. But his gift to her would be with her all her life... The only balm to the endless anguish of her heart.

In the branches of the gnarled apple tree a robin was singing. Far off she could hear a tractor plough-ing a field. The hazy buzz of late bees seeking the last nectar of the year. All of them lulled her...

She felt her eyelids grow heavy, and the garden faded from sight and sound as sleep slipped over her like a soft veil.

Soon another garden filled her dreamscape...with verdant foliage, vivid bougainvillea, a glittering sunlit pool. And Marc was striding towards her. Tall, and strong, and outlined against the cloudless sky. She felt her heart leap with joy…

Her eyes flashed open. Something had woken her. An alien sound. The engine of a car, low and powerful. For a second—a fraction of a second—she remembered the throaty roar of Marc's low-slung monster…the car he'd loved to drive. Then another emotion speared her.

Alarm.

The cottage was down a dead-end lane, leading only to a gate to the fields at the far end. No traffic passed by. So who was it? She was expecting no visitors…

She twisted round to look at the path leading around the side of the cottage to the lane beyond. There was a sudden dizziness in her head…a swirl of vertigo.

Had she turned too fast? Or was it that she had not woken at all, was still dreaming?

Because someone was walking towards her—*striding* towards her. Someone tall and strong, outlined against the cloudless sky. Someone who could not be here—someone she'd thought she would never see again.

But he was in her vision now—searing her retinas, the synapses of her stunned and disbelieving brain. She lurched to her feet and the vertigo hit again.

Or was it shock?

Or waking from the dream?

Or still being within the dream?

She swayed and Marc was there in an instant, steadying her. Then his hands dropped away.

Memory stabbed at her—how he'd made the same gesture in that nightmare encounter at the hotel, dropping his hands from her as if he could not bear to touch her. She clutched at the back of her chair, staring at him, hearing her heart pounding in her veins, feeling disbelief still in her head. And emotion—unbearable emotion—leaping in her heart.

She crushed it down. Whatever he was here for he would tell her and then he would leave.

For one unbearable moment dread knifed in her. *Does he know?*

Oh, dear God, she prayed, please do not let him know! That would be the worst thing of all—the very worst! Because if he did...

She sheared her mind away, forced herself to speak. Heard words fall from her, uncomprehending. 'What...what are you doing here?'

He was standing there and she could see tension in every line of his body. His face was carved as if from tempered steel. As closed as she had ever seen it.

Yet something was different about him—something she had never seen before. Something in the veiling of his eyes that had never been there before.

'I have something to give you,' he said.

His voice was remote. Dispassionate. But, as with the look on his face, she had never heard his voice sound like that.

She stared, confused. 'Wh-what?' she got out.

'This,' he said.

His hand was slipping inside his jacket pocket. He was wearing yet another of his killer suits, she registered abstractedly through the shattering of her mind. Registered, too, the quickening of her pulse, the weakening of her limbs that she always felt with him. Felt the power he had to make her feel like that… Felt the longing that went with it.

Longing she must not let herself feel. No matter that he was standing here, so real, so close…

He was drawing something out from his inner pocket and she caught the silken gleam of the grey lining, the brief flash of the gold fountain pen in the pocket. Then her eyes were only on what he was holding out to her. What she recognised only too well— the slim, elegant jewel case she had returned to him that dreadful day in London that had killed all the last remnants of her hope that he might ever want her again…

She shook her head. Automatically negating.

'Marc—I told you. I can't take it. I know…' She swallowed. 'I know you…you mean well…but you must see that I can't accept it!'

Consternation was filling her. Why was he here? To insist she take those emeralds? She stared at him. His face was still as shuttered as ever, his eyes veiled, unreadable. But a nerve was ticking just below his cheekbone and there were deep lines around his mouth, as though his jaw were steel, filled with tension.

She didn't understand it. All she understood—all that was searing through her like red-hot lava in her veins—was that seeing him again was agony… An agony that had leapt out of the deepest recesses of her being, escaping like a deranged monster to devour her whole.

Through the physical pain rocking her, from holding leashed every muscle in her body, as if she could hold in the anguish blinding her, she heard him speak.

'That is a pity.' He set the case with the emerald necklace in it down on the table beside her chair.

There was still that something different in his voice—that something she'd never heard before. She'd heard ill-humour, short temper, impatience and displeasure. She'd heard desire and passion and warmth and laughter.

But she'd never heard this before.

She stared at him.

He spoke again. 'A pity,' he said, 'because, you see, emeralds would suit you so much better than mere diamonds.'

'I don't understand…' The words fell from her. Bewildered. Hollow.

The very faintest ghost of what surely could not be a twisted smile curved the whipped line of his mouth for an instant. As if he was mocking himself with a savagery that made her take a breath.

'They would suit you so much better than the diamond ring which Hans presented to you.'

Tara struggled to speak. '*Presented?* He *showed* it to me! Dear God, Marc—you could not…? You could not have thought…?'

Disbelief rang in every word that fell from her. He

could *not* have thought that! How *could* he? Shock—more than shock—made her speechless.

A rasp sounded in his throat. It seemed to her that it was torn from somewhere very deep inside him.

'We see what we want to see,' he replied. The mockery was there again, in the twist of his mouth, but the target was only himself. And then there was another emotion in his face. His eyes. 'We see what we *fear* to see.'

She gazed at him, searching his face. Her heart was pounding within her, deafening her. 'I don't understand,' she said again. Her voice was fainter than ever.

'No more did I,' he said. 'I didn't understand at all. Did not understand how I was being made a fool of again. But this time by *myself.*'

She frowned. '"Again"?'

He moved suddenly, restlessly. Not answering her.

Here he was, standing and facing her in this place that had been almost impossible to find—hard to discover even by relentless enquiry.

It had taken him from a ruthless interrogation of her former flatmates, in which he had discovered that she had moved out…had hired a van to transport her belongings, to the tracking down of the hire company, finding out where they had delivered to, and then, finally, to hiring a car of his own and speeding down to that same destination.

All with the devil driving him.

The devil he was purging from himself now, after so many years of its malign possession. So much depended on it. *All* depended on it.

He took a breath—a ragged breath. 'When you look at me, Tara, what do you see?'

What do you see?

His words echoed in her skull. Crying out for an answer she must not give.

I see the man I love, who has never loved me! I see the man who did not want me, though I still want him—and always will, for all my days! That is the man I see—and I cannot tell you that! I cannot tell you because you don't want me as I want you, and I will not burden you with my wanting you. I will not burden you with the love you do not want from me... Nor with the gift you gave me.

But silence held her—as it must. Whatever he had come here for, it was not to hear her break the stricken silence that she must keep.

He spoke again, in that same low, demanding tone.

'Do you see a man rich and powerful in his own realm of worldly wealth? A man who can command the luxuries of life? Who has others to do his bidding, whatever he wants of them? Whose purpose is to protect the heritage he was born to—to protect the wealth he possesses, to guard it from all who might want to seize it from him?' His voice changed now. 'To guard it from all who might want to make a fool of him?'

He shifted again, restless still, then his voice continued. Eyes flashing back to her.

'You saw Celine with Hans—you saw how she took ruthless advantage of him, wanted him only for his wealth. You saw what she did to him—' He made a noise of scorn and disgust in his throat. 'I am richer than Hans—considerably so, if all our accounts were pitted one against the other! But...' He took a savage breath. 'I am as vulnerable as he is.' A twisted, self-mocking smile taunted his mouth. 'The only difference is that I know it. Know it and guard endlessly against it.' He shook his head. 'I guard myself against every woman I encounter.'

His expression changed.

'And the way I do it is very simple—I keep to women from my own world. Women who have wealth of their own...who therefore will not covet mine. It was a strategy that worked until—' he took a ravaged breath, his eyes boring into hers, to make her understand '—until I encountered you.'

A raw breath incised his lungs.

'I broke a lifetime's rules for you, Tara! I knew it was rash, unwise, but I could not resist it! Could not resist *you*. You taunted me with your beauty, with that mouthy lip of yours, daring to prick my *amour propre*! Answering me back...defying me! And your worst crime of all...' His voice was changing too, and he could not stop it doing so. It was softening into a sensual tone that was echoing the quickening of his pulse, the sweep of his lashes over his eyes. 'You denied me what I wanted—pushing me away, telling me it was only play-acting, tormenting me with it.'

His breath was ragged again, his eyes burning into hers.

'And so when we were *finally* alone together, free of that damnable role-play, I could only think that I should not make it real with you—that I should not break my lifetime's rules…'

He saw her face work, her eyes shadow.

'Not all women are like Celine, Marc.'

Her voice was sad. Almost pitying. It was a pity he could not bear.

He gave a harsh laugh. 'But they *could* be! And how am I to *tell*? How would I *know*?' He paused, and then with a hardening of his face continued. 'I thought I knew once. I was young, and arrogant and so, so sure of myself—and of the woman I wanted. Who seemed to want me too. Until…' He could not look at her, could see only the past, indelible in his memory, a warning throughout his life, 'Until the day I saw her across a restaurant, wearing the engagement ring of a man far older than I. Far richer—'

He tore his voice away and he forced his eyes to go back to the woman who stood in his present, not in his past.

'How could I *know*?' he repeated. His eyes rested on her, impassive, veiling what he would not show. 'That last night you asked to come with me to New York…'

She blenched, he could see the colour draining from her skin, but he could not stop now.

'But if you came to New York with me then where next? Back to Paris? To move in with me perhaps? For how long? What would you want? What would you start to take for granted?' His voice changed, and there was a coldness in it he could not keep out. 'What would you start to expect as your due?'

He drew breath again.

'That's why I ended it between us,' he said. 'That's why,' he went on, and he knew there was a deadness in his voice, 'I left you the emerald necklace. Sent you that cheque. To…to draw a line under whatever had been. What you might have thought there was— or could be.'

He fell silent.

Tara could hear his breathing, hear her own. Had heard the truth he'd spoken. She pulled her shoulders back, straightening her spine, letting her hands fall to her side. Lifted her chin. Looked him in the eye. She was not the daughter of soldiers for nothing.

'I never thought it, Marc.' Her voice was blank. Remote. 'I never thought there was anything more between us than what we had.'

She had said it. And it was not a lie. It was simply not all the truth. Between 'thought' and 'hope' was a distance so vast it shrank the universe to an atom.

'But I did,' he said. His jaw clenched. 'I did think it.' His expression changed. 'I didn't want to end it, Tara. I didn't want *us* to end. But…' Something flashed in his face. 'But I was afraid.'

She saw a frown crease his forehead, as if he had encountered a problem he had not envisaged. As if he were seeing it for the first time in his life.

'But what is the point of fear,' he asked, as if to the universe itself, 'if it destroys our only chance of happiness?'

His eyes went to her now, and in them, yet again, was something she had never seen before. She could not name it, yet it called to her from across a chasm as wide as all the world. And as narrow as the space between them.

She saw his hand go to the jewel case, flick it open. Green fire glittered within.

'Emeralds would suit you,' he said again, 'so much better than mere diamonds. Which is why—'

There was a constriction in his voice—she could hear it…could feel her heart start to slug within her. Hard and heavy beats, like a tattoo inside her body.

She saw him replace the necklace on the table, saw his hand slide once again within his breast pocket, draw out another object. A cube this time, with the same crest on it that the emerald necklace case held. She saw him flick it open. Saw what was within.

He extended his hand towards her, the ring in its box resting in his palm. 'It's yours if you want it,' he said. The casualness of the words belied the taut-ness of his jaw, the nerve flickering in his cheek-bone, the sudden veiling of his eyes as if to protect himself. 'Along with one other item, should it be of any value to you.'

The drumming of her heartbeat was rising up in-side her, deafening in volume. Her throat thickened so she could not breathe.

He glanced at her again, and there was a sudden tensing in his expression that hollowed his face, made it gaunt with strain. 'It's my heart, Tara. It comes with the ring if you want it—'

A hand flew to her mouth, stifling a cry in her tearing throat. 'Marc! No! Don't say it—oh, don't say it! Not if…not if you don't mean it!' Fear was in her face, terror. 'I couldn't bear it—'

Her fingers pressed against her mouth, making her words almost inaudible, but he could hear them all the same.

'It's too late,' he said. 'I've said it now. I can't take it back. I can't take back anything—anything at all! Not a single thing I've ever said to you—not a single kiss, a single heartbeat.' Emotion scythed across his face. 'It's too late for everything,' he said. 'Too late for fear.'

He lifted his free hand, gently drew back the fingers pressing against her mouth, folding his own around her, strong and warm.

'What good would it do me? Fear? I can gather all the proof I want—the fact that you returned my cheque, refused my emeralds, gave away a couture wardrobe! That my insane presumption that you had helped me dispose of Celine only to clear the path for your own attempt on Hans was nothing more than the absurd creation of my fears. But there *is* no proof! No proof that can withstand the one sure truth of all.'

He pressed her fingers, turning them over in his hand, exposing the delicate skin of her wrist. He dipped his head to let his lips graze like silken velvet, with sensuous softness… Then he lifted his head, poured his gaze into hers.

Her eyes glimmered with tears, emotion swelling within her like a wondrous wave. Could this be true? Really true?

'Will you take my heart?' he was saying now. 'For it holds the one sure truth of all.'

His eyes moved on her face, as if searching…finding.

'It's *love*, Tara. That's the only one sure truth. All that I can rely on—all that I need to rely on. For if you should love me then I am safe. Safe from all my fear.'

His eyes were filled with all she had longed to see in them.

'And if my love for you should be of any value to you—'

Another choking cry came from her and her arm flung itself around his neck, clutching him to her. Words flew from her. 'I've tried so hard—so desperately hard—to let you go! Oh, not from my life—I knew that you were over in my life—but in my heart. Oh, dear God, I could not tear you from my heart…'

The truth that she would have silenced all her life, never burdening him with it, broke from her now, and sobs—endless sobs that seemed to last for ever—discharged all that she had forced herself to keep buried deep within her, unacknowledged, silent and smothered.

As he wrapped her arm around her waist, pressing it tightly to him, something tumbled from his palm. But he did not notice. It was not important. Only this had any meaning…only this was precious.

To have Tara in his arms again. Tara whom he'd thrown away, let go, lost.

He had let fear possess him. Destroy his only chance of happiness in life.

He soothed her now, murmuring soft words, until her weeping eased and ebbed and she took a trembling step back from him. He gazed down at her. Her eyes were red from crying, tear runnels stained her cheeks, her mouth was wobbly and uneven, her features contorted still…

The most beautiful woman in the world.

'I once took it upon myself to announce that you were my fiancée,' he said, his voice wry and his eyes with a dark glint in them. 'But now…' His voice changed again, and with a little rush of emotion she heard uncertainty in his voice, saw a questioning doubt in his eyes about her answer to what he was saying. 'Now I take nothing upon myself at all.' He paused, searching her eyes. 'So tell me—I beg you… implore you—if I proposed to you now, properly, as a suitor should, would you say yes?'

She burst into tears once more. He drew her to him again, muffled her cries in his shoulder, and then he was soothing her yet again, murmuring more words to her, until once again she eased her tears and drew tremblingly back.

'Dare I keep talking?' he put to her.

She gave another choke, but it was of laughter as well as tears. Her gaze was misty, but in it he saw all that he had hoped beyond hope to see.

He bent to kiss her mouth—a soft, tender kiss, that calmed all the violent emotion that had been shaken from her, leaving her a peace inside her that was vast and wondrous. Could this be true and real? Or only the figment of her longings?

But it *was* real! Oh, so real. And he was here, and kissing her…kissing her for ever and ever…

And then he was drawing back, frowning, looking around him.

'What is it?' Tara asked, her voice still trembling, her whole body swaying with the emotion consuming her.

He frowned. 'I had a ring here somewhere,' he said. 'I need it—'

She glanced down, past where the emerald necklace lay on the garden table in its box, into the grass beneath. Something glinted greener than the grass. She gave a little cry of discovery and he swooped to pick it up from where it had fallen.

He possessed himself of her hand, which trembled like the rest of her. Slid the ring over her finger. Then he raised her hand to his lips, turned it over in his palm. Lowered his mouth to kiss the tender skin over the veins in her wrist. A kiss of tenderness, of homage.

Then he folded her hand within his own. 'I knew that I had gone way past mere desire for you,' he said, his voice low, intense, his eyes holding hers with a gaze that made her heart turn over, 'when on the evening of the bank's autumn client party—which Hans always comes to—I realised that for all the blackness in my heart over what I thought you had done, there was only one emotion in me.'

He paused, and she felt his hands clench over hers.

'It was an unbearable longing for you,' he said, and there was a catch in his voice that made Tara press his hands with hers, placing her free hand over his.

'As unbearable as my longing to see my parents again after their deaths—'

He broke off and she slipped her hands from his, slid them around him, drawing her to him. She held him close and tight and for ever. Moved beyond all things by what he had said.

Then, suddenly, he was pulling away from her.

'Tara…' His voice was hollow. Hollow with shock.

Her expression changed as she realised what he had discovered. And she knew she must tell him why she had made the agonising decision that she had.

'You didn't want me, Marc,' she said quietly. Sadly. 'So I would never, *never* have forced this on you.'

He let his hands drop, stepped back a moment. His face was troubled.

'Are you angry?'

He heard the note of fear in her voice. 'Only at myself,' he said. 'My fears nearly cost me my life's happiness,' he said. His voice was sombre, grave. Self-accusing. 'And they nearly cost me even more.' His face worked, and then in the same sombre voice he spoke again. 'I tried to find proof—proof that you did not value my wealth above myself.' He took a ragged breath. 'But if I wanted the greatest proof of all it is this. That you were prepared to raise my baby by yourself…never telling me, never claiming a single *sou* from me—'

Her voice was full as she answered him. 'I could not have borne it if you had felt any…any *obligation*. Of any kind.' She drew breath. 'But now…'

She smiled and took his hand in hers again. Slowly,

carefully, she placed it across her gently swelling waistline. She saw wonder fill his face, light in his eyes, and her heart lifted to soar.

French words broke from him, raw and heartfelt. She leant to kiss his mouth. There was a glint in her eye now. 'I'm going to lose my figure, you know… Turn into a barrage balloon. You won't desire me any more—not for months and months and months!'

The familiar look was in his eyes—that oh-so-familiar look that melted the bones of her body.

'I will *always* desire you!' he promised, and he laughed. Joy was soaring in him, like eagles taking flight. And desire too—heating him from within.

She gave a laugh of pure happiness that lifted her from her feet—or was it Marc, sweeping her up into his arms?

She gave a choke, felt emotion wringing her. 'Marc, is this real? *Is* it? Tell me it is! Because I can't be this happy—how *can* I?'

The future that had loomed before her—empty of all but the most precious memento of her brief time with him—now flowed and merged with the past she had lost…becoming an endless present that she knew she would never lose!

His arms tightened around her, his eyes pouring into hers. 'As real as it is for me,' he said.

Happiness such as he had never known since the carefree days of his youth overflowed in him. Tara was his for ever, and she was bringing to him a gift that was a wonder and a joy to him: the baby that was to be born.

He was striding with her now, towards the cottage. He glanced around, as if seeing it for the first time. 'Is this the new life you said you were making for yourself?'

She smiled, tightening her grip around his neck with the hook of her arm. 'A new life—and an old one,' she said. 'The cottage belonged to my grandparents, and they left it to me. It's always been my haven…'

'And it will be ours, too, if you will permit me to share it with you,' he said, his voice warm. 'In fact it seems to me that it would be the ideal place for a honeymoon…'

The glint in his eyes was melting her bones as he negotiated the narrow doorway, sweeping her indoors and ducking his tall frame beneath the beamed lintel. Purposefully, he headed for the stairs. There must be bedrooms upstairs, and beds…

He dropped a kiss on her mouth as he carried her aloft, following her hurried directions to her bedroom, lowering her down upon the old-fashioned brass bed which creaked under their combined weight, sinking them deep into the feather mattress.

'Starting right now.'

'Now, that…' Tara sighed blissfully '…is a *wonderful* idea!'

Marc gave a growl of satisfaction at her answer and began to remove their entirely unnecessary clothing, covering her face in kisses that would last their lifetimes—and beyond.

EPILOGUE

MARC STOOD ON the terrace of the Villa Derenz, his infant son cradled in his arms. Out on the manicured lawn, under the shade of a huge parasol beside the pool, Tara dozed on a lounger.

His eyes went to her, soft with love-light. Here she had first beguiled him and entranced him, lighting a flame within him that his own fears had so nearly extinguished but which now burnt with everlasting fire.

He walked up to her, feeling the warmth of late summer lapping him. At his approach she roused herself and smiled, holding out her arms expectantly.

'Afternoon tea is served, young Master Derenz!' she said, and laughed, busying herself settling him to feed.

Marc dropped a lingering kiss on her forehead, then turned as two figures of military bearing emerged from the villa, coming towards him and Tara.

'Feeding him up? Good, good…' Major Mackenzie nodded approvingly at his grandson's nursing.

'Latched on properly?' the other Major Mackenzie asked her daughter.

'Mum, I'm not one of your subalterns,' Tara remonstrated good-humouredly, with a laugh, patting the lounger for her mother to sit down beside her.

Her parents had welcomed the news of their daughter's marriage with open delight, and her mother had organised the wedding at the little parish church near the cottage with military precision. Her father had even summoned a guard of honour for the bride and groom, formed by the men of his regiment.

And if a tear had moistened her mother's eyes, only Tara had seen it, and only she had heard her mother say, with more emotion in her voice than her daughter was used to hearing, 'He can't take his eyes off you, that utterly gorgeous man of yours! And he is lucky—*so lucky*—to have you!' Then she had hugged her daughter closely.

The arrival of their grandson had also persuaded her parents to return to Civvy Street, and they would soon buy a house on the Dorset coast, near enough to for them to keep an eye on the cottage. Tara was glad for them and glad for herself—she would be seeing more of them, and they were safe from future military deployment.

She was also glad that Marc's son would have grandparents on her side to grow up with. But there would be happy memories in the making here, too, at the villa on Cap Pierre, just as Marc had from his own boyhood with his parents and their friends.

The Neubergers, with Hans's new grandchild on

the way, would soon be here to spend a fortnight, after her parents had returned to the UK. Hans had not been slow to express his gladness that Marc and she were so happy together.

She looked up lovingly at her husband and he met her gaze, his dark eyes softening, his heart catching.

How can I love her so much? How is it possible?

All he knew was that he did, and that theirs was a love that would never end. And to have found it made him the most fortunate man in the world.

There was the sound of a throat clearing and he glanced across at his father-in-law.

'If it's all right with you, old chap,' said Major Mackenzie, 'we'd like to take out that very neat little boat of yours! Wind's rising, and we're keen to try out the spinnaker.'

Marc smiled broadly. 'An excellent idea,' he said warmly, and Tara added her own encouragement.

Her mother rose briskly to her feet and she and Marc watched them stride across the lawn to the path leading to the jetty, where the boat was moored.

'You could go out with them too, you know,' she said to Marc.

He shook his head. 'I was thinking, actually, of a quite different activity. When, that is, young Master Derenz requires his afternoon nap…'

Tara's eyes glinted knowingly. 'And what might that be, Monsieur Derenz?' she enquired limpidly.

He gave a low laugh. 'Well, Madame Derenz, I was thinking,' he said, returning the glint in her eye with a deeper one of his own, 'that perhaps it is time to consider the addition of a Mademoiselle Derenz to the family...'

She caught his hand and kissed it. 'An *excellent* idea,' she agreed. 'Happy families...' She sighed. 'It just doesn't get better.'

And Marc could not help but agree—with all his heart.

* * * * *

If you enjoyed
Billionaire's Mediterranean Proposal
you're sure to enjoy these other stories
by Julia James!

Carrying His Scandalous Heir
The Greek's Secret Son
Tycoon's Ring of Convenience
Heiress's Pregnancy Scandal

Available now!

COMING NEXT MONTH FROM

HARLEQUIN

Presents.

Available May 21, 2019

#3721 THE SHEIKH CROWNS HIS VIRGIN
Billionaires at the Altar
by Lynne Graham
When Zoe is kidnapped, she's saved by Raj—an exiled desert prince. The attraction between them is instant! Yet her rescue comes with a price: to avoid a scandal, Zoe *must* become Raj's virgin bride...

#3722 SHOCK HEIR FOR THE KING
Secret Heirs of Billionaires
by Clare Connelly
Frankie is shocked when Matt, the stranger she gave her innocence to, reappears. Now she's in for the biggest shock of all—he's actually *King* Matthias! And to claim his heir, he demands Frankie become his queen!

#3723 GREEK'S BABY OF REDEMPTION
One Night With Consequences
by Kate Hewitt
When brooding billionaire Alex needs a wife to secure his business, his housekeeper, Milly, agrees. But their wedding night sparks an unexpected fire... Could Milly—and his unborn child—be the key to Alex's redemption?

#3724 UNTOUCHED UNTIL HER ULTRA-RICH HUSBAND
by Dani Collins
To avoid destitution, Luli needs outrageously wealthy Gabriel's help. The multi-billionaire's solution? He'll secure both their futures by marrying her! But after sweeping Luli into his luxurious world, Gabriel discovers the chemistry with his untouched wife is *priceless*...

HPCNM0519RA

#3725 A SCANDALOUS MIDNIGHT IN MADRID
Passion in Paradise
by Susan Stephens

A moonlit encounter tempts Sadie all the way to Alejandro's castle...and into his bed! But their night of illicit pleasure soon turns Sadie into Spain's most scandalous headline: *Pregnant with Alejandro's baby!*

#3726 UNTAMED BILLIONAIRE'S INNOCENT BRIDE
Conveniently Wed!
by Caitlin Crews

To prevent a scandal, Lauren needs to find reclusive Dominik—her boss's estranged brother—and convince him to marry her! As Dominik awakens her long-dormant desire, will Lauren accept that their hunger can't be denied?

#3727 CLAIMING HIS REPLACEMENT QUEEN
Monteverre Marriages
by Amanda Cinelli

Khalil's motivation for marriage is politics, not passion. Yet a sizzling encounter with his soon-to-be queen, Cressida, changes everything. And the desire innocent Cressida ignites is too hot to resist...

#3728 REUNITED BY THE GREEK'S VOWS
by Andie Brock

Kate is stunned when ex-fiancé, Nikos, storms back into her life—and demands they marry! Desperate to save her company, she agrees. But what these heated adversaries don't anticipate is that their still-smoldering flame will explode into irresistible passion...

YOU CAN FIND MORE INFORMATION ON UPCOMING HARLEQUIN® TITLES, FREE EXCERPTS AND MORE AT WWW.HARLEQUIN.COM.

HPCNM0519RB

SPECIAL EXCERPT FROM

⟨H⟩ HARLEQUIN *Presents*®

> *To avoid destitution, Luli needs outrageously wealthy*
> *Gabriel's help. The multibillionaire's solution? He'll*
> *secure both their futures by marrying her! But sweeping*
> *Luli into his luxurious world, Gabriel discovers the*
> *chemistry with his untouched wife is priceless...*

Read on for a sneak preview of
Dani Collins's next story,
Untouched Until Her Ultra-Rich Husband!

You told me what you were worth, Luli. Act like you believe it.

She had been acting. The whole time. Still was, especially as a handful of designers whose names she knew from Mae's glossy magazines behaved with deference as they welcomed her to a private showroom complete with catwalk.

She had to fight back laughing with incredulity as they offered her champagne, caviar, even a pedicure.

"I—" She glanced at Gabriel, expecting him to tell them she aspired to model and should be treated like a clotheshorse, not royalty.

"A full wardrobe," he said. "Top to bottom, morning to night, office to evening. Do what you can overnight, then send the rest to my address in New York."

"Mais bien sûr, monsieur," the couturier said without a hint of falter in her smile. "Our pleasure."

"Gabriel—" Luli started to protest as the women scattered.

"You remember what I said about this?" He tapped the wallet that held her phone. "I need you to stay on brand."

"Reflect who you are?"

"Yes."

"Who are you?" she asked ruefully. "I only met you ten minutes ago."

"I'm a man who doesn't settle for anything less than the best." He touched her chin. "The world is going to have a lot of questions about why we married. Give them an answer."

HPEXP0519

His words roused the competitor who still lurked inside her. She wanted to prove to the world she was worthy to be his wife. Maybe she wanted to prove her worth to him, too. Definitely she longed to prove something to herself.

Either way, she made sure those long-ago years of preparation paid off. She had always been ruthless in evaluating her own shortcomings and knew how to play to her strengths. She might not be trying to win a crown today, but she hadn't been then, either. She'd been trying to win the approval of a woman who hadn't deserved her idolatry.

She pushed aside those dark memories and clung instead to the education she had gained in those difficult years.

"That neckline will make my shoulders look narrow," she said, making quick up-and-down choices. "The sweetheart style is better, but no ruffles at my hips. Don't show me yellow. Tangerine is better. A more verdant green. That one is too pale." In her head, she was sectioning out the building blocks of a cohesive stage presence. Youthful, but not too trendy. Sensual, but not overtly sexual. Charismatic without being showy.

"Something tells me I'm not needed," Gabriel said twenty minutes in and rose to leave. "We'll go for dinner in three hours." He glanced to the couturier. "And return in the morning for another fitting."

"Parfait. Merci, monsieur." Her smile was calm, but the way people were bustling told Luli how big a deal this was. How big a deal Gabriel was.

The women took her measurements while showing her unfinished pieces that only needed hemming or minimal tailoring so she could take them immediately.

"You'll be up all night," Luli murmured to one of the seamstresses.

The young woman moved quickly, but not fast enough for her boss, who kept crying, *"Vite! Vite!"*

"I'm sorry to put you through this," Luli added.

"Pas de problème. Monsieur Dean is a treasured client. It's our honor to provide your trousseau." She clamped her teeth on a pin between words. "Do you know where he's taking you for dinner? We should choose that dress next, so I can work on the alterations while you have your hair and makeup done. It must be fabulous. The world will be watching."

She would be presented publicly as his wife, Luli realized with a hard thump in her heart.

Don't miss
Untouched Until Her Ultra-Rich Husband.
*Available June 2019 wherever
Harlequin® Presents books and ebooks are sold.*

www.Harlequin.com

HPEXP0519